BECAUSE HE'S WATCHING IAN'S
OBSESSION
KENNY WRIGHT

KW PUBLISHING
www.kennywriter.com

Because He's Watching: Ian's Obsession

FOREWORD

I first "met" Kenny when he sent me an email about one of my stories. I don't even remember which one it was, but that led me to check out his work and I found he was quite a talented writer in his own right. This led to a longstanding friendship and you could probably say Kenny is my second husband because I "talk" to him—by email—more than any other man save my husband. Luckily, my real life husband is not the jealous type. I hope his wife doesn't mind when I need to "borrow" her husband. That sounds like the plot for one of our books! I soon learned that not only is Kenny a talented writer, but an excellent graphic designer. He's designed almost all of my covers—certainly the best ones—since I started self-publishing. All you have to do is look down a list of my ebooks to see a gallery of his awesome work.

Over the years, Kenny has become not only a good friend, but a trusted voice when it comes to my writing. I know my characters have grown deeper because of his thoughts on my work. Writers can get into our own heads when it comes to our work and we need someone who will be honest about what we've written. We need someone who will tell us, "No, that's a terrible idea," or "Try this, not that." Kenny is that for me.

Kenny first showed me what would become *Because He's Watching: Ian's Obsession* in the early stages, I think maybe the first two chapters were finished. I loved the concept of a man who sets down a potentially self-destructive path after a chance meeting provides him with the opportunity to fulfill one of his wildest, darkest fantasies about his wife. It could very easily become a be-careful-what-you-wish-for story. The key was to always keep it centered on the couple, Ian and Emily. With such a fertile set-up, I couldn't help but wonder what Ian's wife, Emily, must be thinking when her husband encourages her to flirt with—then push even further—with her hunky younger co-worker. Wouldn't Emily think her husband was out of his mind? Would she be able to admit—even to herself—that this might be something she wanted too—that it wasn't just for her husband. When I shared these thoughts with Kenny, he generously suggested that I tackle the tale from Emily's point of view, and my own novel, *Because He's Watching* was born.

We collaborated on the plot, and since we have different sensibilities—Kenny is a romantic, the eternal optimist; I'm inclined to think playing with fire must have consequences—things got rocky at times, but by marrying our two visions we came up with a rich, complicated story of a couple that plays with opening their marriage and facing what that might mean for their relationship. I don't think either character, Kenny's Ian or my Emily, turned out to be exactly who we thought they'd be, because we each forced the other to think about who these people really were.

In the end, Kenny had more thinking to do on who Ian was, so *Because He's Watching* was published first, to a receptive audience. Kenny moved onto other projects, but he's finally come back to Ian and a couple years away has given him a fresh, interesting perspective on what makes Ian tick. *Because He's Watching: Ian's Obsession* is an interesting take on what happens to a man when he indulges his darkest desire. What is it like to watch your wife with another man? How does it really feel to watch her kiss and touch him? Can you ever look at her in the same way afterward? Kenny is a master in this wife-watching subgenre of Erotica, but this may be his most complex look at an obsessed husband yet. It's definitely something any fan of my own *Because He's Watching* should read. I only told half the story. This is the other side.

Kirsten McCurran, December 2013

INTRODUCTION

I could stop her. It wasn't too late. She was still there, not twenty feet away. I looked at the door; felt its pull. Instead, all I could think about was that stupid saying: *be careful what you wish for...*

The last couple weeks flashed by, and in looking back, I'd been anything but *careful*. It was an obsession, I realized only now, at the end. But that's how it is in the moment, right? The decisions were small ones until they weren't—until I could no longer fool myself into thinking that life would be the same.

I stood at the window as Emily glanced one last time in my direction, offered a shy wave, and stepped into her Prius.

Be careful what you wish for, because you might just get it.

As mad with jealousy as it made me, God, I hoped so.

CHAPTER 1

Two weeks earlier...

The crack of colliding pool balls and the pleasant murmur of conversation were my first impressions of Bar 88. It was early still and the sparse crowd of after work businessmen and women looked like a beer commercial ready to happen. I got the feeling that it was only waiting for the six o'clock hour.

I settled in at the bar and ordered a beer, despite the long list of happy hour cocktails and the towering display of top shelf liquor. This was as good a place as any to grab a drink, and after today's fruitless meetings, I needed one or two.

The ambiance was upscale. Bar 88 was the type of suburban neighborhood bar that the yuppies hung out at. A handful of pool tables were sprinkled throughout the lower level while the upper floor, high in the unfinished rafters, was more of a dining area that overlooked the bar. It looked empty, although again, it was early.

Two of the billiard tables were occupied, one by a rowdy group of college guys, the other by a solitary player who looked like another escapee from the office. Like me, he wore the remains of the workday like scraps of armor: trousers that had picked up wrinkles, a tie-less and fitted oxford with the shirt-sleeves rolled up his forearms, a Blackberry clipped to his belt.

He was about ten years younger, maybe in his late twenties or early thirties, and built in a way I never was. His thick arms bulged under his rolled sleeves and his barrel chest spoke of time spent in the gym. A military crew-cut completed his look and while he did not look at all like someone I would hang out with, I just couldn't shake the feeling that I knew him. He was shooting alone, working the table with determined focus, and based on the number of scratches and missed shots, he was in the early stages of learning the game.

It took half my beer to place him. I couldn't recall his name, but I was pretty sure he worked with my wife, Emily. That was it. I'd seen him in a couple of photographs she'd shown me from office events and I seemed to recall him being introduced as one of the new employees at the last Christmas party.

I decided to join him. I still had a few hours to kill due my disaster of a meeting. I hadn't played pool in forever and it seemed like a good idea at the time. Little did I know...

"Hey there," I said as I walked up to his table.

The man turned to me, the pool stick by his side, and stared at me without recognition. "Hey," he replied after a beat.

Okay, so he didn't recognize me, but that was fair since I still didn't remember his name. I made a snap decision to chat with him, figuring I might learn some embarrassing stories about my wife I could use to tease her later. It's not every day you get an insight into what your other half is like when you're not around.

"You're not bad. Want to split a few games?" I asked.

It must have come off as oddly forward from a stranger. I could see the wheels turning as he tried to figure out if I was trying to pick him up or hustle him. He must have decided to trust me because he shrugged and said, "Why not? Want to play for who pays?" He had a crisp voice, though not as deep as I'd expected.

"Perfect." I set my beer down and picked out a pool cue.

"I'm Ray," he offered as he racked the balls. "I haven't seen you around here..."

Still didn't remember me and an idea flashed through my mind.

"Neil," I greeted, exchanging a hard handshake. For the life of me, I have no idea where that came from, or why I did it. I told myself I would get better stories about Emily if he didn't know I was her husband. This first lie started me down a slippery slope.

Ray was about three inches taller and had an easy, quick smile that I imagined women responded well to. He was handsome in that generic, all-American way.

"Actually, this is my first time here. Was in the neighborhood for a meeting and, well, we were thrown out. The others decided to take the day off and go home, but it was my project. I need a drink."

"Sorry to hear that. Why don't I get the first round?"

I set the racked balls on the green felt and smirked. "What makes you think you won't be anyway, when I beat you?"

"Fair enough." Again, that grin.

We shot around a little and neither of us was very good. We chit-chatted while we played and I had the oddest feeling, like I was playing with fire. What did I really think I would hear about my Emily? I asked if this was his usual haunt.

"Yeah, I come here pretty often. I've recently gotten into pool, and there's usually a table open on the weekdays. It's not a bad place and the Happy Hour prices are pretty reasonable, despite the neighborhood."

A pretty brunette barmaid in her early twenties passed by, wearing a short, cut-off jean skirt and a halter top that did little to hide her full breasts. "Nice staff, too," I commented as I watched her put in an order at the bar.

Ray gave a chuckle. "There's that, too, although she's a little young for me."

"Like them older?"

Ray laughed again, taking his turn to sink a few balls. "You know, sometimes a little experience can go a long way."

We talked about the neighborhood and what we did for work. Other than the bit about my name, I kept things truthful. I was an architect in the city. I had two kids, was married for close to ten years. Ray told me he worked as a technical writer at TNK, where Emily also works, and was single, with no girlfriend or kids and had a place in the city. He liked his life and wasn't ready to settle down quite yet, but it did seem like he felt he was lagging behind his peers.

"There was a phase when all my friends were getting married. I went to a wedding every month, it seemed. Now, it's baby showers," he said

"I remember those days."

"Not for me. Not yet, anyway. I'm still having fun."

"The crazy life of a single, young technical writer," I joked. "Probably not much eye-candy at work. I can see why you need to unwind here."

My wife was one of only two women in her department who wasn't an administrative assistant.

"You'd be surprised."

"Yeah?" I asked. "Is there a lot of ass over there at TNK? I've got a buddy who works IT for you guys and he always talks about the women he sees when he needs to come up and fix something." I figured it was a safe lie, since in my experience most IT guys get ignored.

"There are a few, actually."

"Oh yeah? Who's the hottest chick in your office?"

I couldn't believe I was going down this road. The plan was to find out something embarrassing about Emily, not find out if the guys in her office had the hots for her. I didn't stop him, though. It would be kind of exciting to hear some other guy talk about my wife the way guys do.

Ray didn't even hesitate. "One of them puts apple-cheeks over there to shame."

"Now I'm intrigued..." I didn't dare think ahead. Not one second.

"You should be!" Ray shot a ball into the corner pocket with force. "Light eyes and dark hair. Nice body. A real natural beauty. God, I love that look."

"Me too." My stomach fluttered. I could barely trust myself to speak. Emily. He had to be talking about Emily.

He didn't stop. I didn't stop him. "She's got a body to match. About five-five or so, with the perkiest set of tits." He held his hands out as though grasping Emily's full B-cups. "She works out every day at lunch at a gym around the corner from the office. Hell, I started doing the same, just to watch her sweat in those tight little outfits of hers. If I've ever seen a more perfect ass..." He shook his head.

I'd gone fishing for compliments for my wife and pulled up a whale. I was happy to be fortified by alcohol or this would have been difficult. I should have been offended to hear him talk about my wife that way, right? Unfortunately, the alcohol also made it impossible to keep myself from digging deeper.

"You ever hit that?"

Why the hell did I ask that? Emily would never cheat on me! How did I keep my voice so even when I felt like such a mess? I held the pool cue with both hands to keep them from shaking.

Ray laughed, shaking his head. "Nah. I mean, we flirt, but nothing beyond that. She's married."

"Don't tell me that's stopped you in the past." What the hell was I saying?

"Hey, I respect the institution of marriage…most of the time." He leaned on his pool cue, grinning wide. "Sometimes, when we're talking, dude, all I can think about is her riding me, that tight little body of hers bouncing up and down on me… But anyway, if there's one thing I'm going to regret when I move, it's probably that chick."

"Oh? You moving?"

"In two weeks. Up to Philly."

I licked my lips. I spoke before I could stop myself. "Then you've got nothing to lose. In two weeks, you'll be gone. I say go for it."

"You may have point," he said.

Oh God, was I really doing this? Was I really talking this guy into going after my wife? My mouth kept opening and closing, and words kept pouring out.

"How long has she been married? You know?"

"Forever and a day, I think. Couple kids, too."

"Well, then there's probably not much excitement left there. It's probably all sex once a month and only in the dark."

Ray shrugged. "I doubt that. She's still hot after two kids and any woman who keeps herself in shape like that is a goer." He finished his beer and signaled for another pitcher. "Emily's wild under that conservative exterior. C'mon, you know the type."

Hearing Ray say her name was like a slap to the face. There was no doubt about it now. He was talking about my wife. And he did seem to have a real line on what she's like. My darker side charged full bore ahead.

"Sure. So you think she's like that?"

I'd gone digging. Was a prepared for what I found? Emily had always been the ultimate girl-next-door: warm and charming and pretty, proper and well behaved. That Ray thought differently was a shock—although a very stimulating one.

"I know women. She has all the signs."

The signs? What signs?

"It's just the way she presents herself. She wears these tailored business suits, right? Always looks professional, with the perfect hair and make-up. But underneath, well... Let's just say I've caught glimpses of the woman beneath the suit. Sometimes there's the line of her thong under a tight skirt, or the lacy top of a stocking, or if I'm really lucky she leans forward just a little too far and you can see down her blouse. I'm not the only one who's noticed, believe me. We're always on the lookout for a piece."

Emily did enjoy sexy lingerie, although I had to admit it had been a long time since I'd paid much attention to it. The stockings were a bit of a surprise though, since she'd always complained whenever I'd asked her to wear them for me, even though I know wearing them made her feel sexy.

"And then there were the few times she's gone out to happy hour with us," Ray went on. "The business exterior melts. She undoes a couple of those buttons on her blouse and really loosens up. You know what I mean."

Did I? "Sounds like an interesting lady."

Ray nodded. "You've got that right. She's been in a relationship so long that maybe she's forgotten what getting all hot and heavy is like. All women like to be swept off their feet, you know, get caught up in the moment and throw caution to the wind."

"Has she?" I croaked and sipped my beer. "I mean, thrown caution to the wind?"

"Not yet, but I think I see it there, the gleam in her eye, that she wants to. Maybe she just needs a little push," he said thoughtfully.

"And maybe you're the one to push her," I said.

Oh God, what had I done?

Even as half of me freaked out at what I'd just done, the other half rationalized that he had to be wrong. He had to be projecting, seeing what he wanted to see because he wanted to screw her.

"I'd better hit the road, it being a school night and all."

"Yeah, I need to get out of here too," Ray agreed. We shook. "I usually shoot on my own, but it was fun hanging out and having some guy talk."

"Yeah, it was. Maybe I'll see you around. You can tell me more about this piece of ass Emily."

"Yeah, that'd be cool. Hopefully next time, I'll have something to share. I'm usually here after work. Stop by anytime."

CHAPTER 2

I got in my car—a bad idea, considering the amount I'd had to drink—and drove home. It was the least reckless thing I'd done so far, I figured, and if I died, who cared?

Reviewing the facts drunkenly, I concluded that this had definitely been a fun little exercise. There was no real harm done, after all. Emily was a loving wife as always, and my own sense of pride was stroked by listening to a stranger talk about how attractive she was.

Then my mind flashed to some of things Ray actually said. *One of them puts apple-cheeks over there to shame...Watching her ride me...*

I'd been here before. No use denying the drunken mind.

A year ago.

At my nephew's wedding.

I'd watched Emily dance with some of the groomsmen, all about Ray's age, all handsome in their youth. When Emily had spotted me watching her, she'd returned, shyly, and asked if I was upset with her. I wasn't. More than that, I was strangely turned on by it. I'd blown out my knee and couldn't dance, so I'd encouraged her to have fun.

Throughout the night, she floated from one set of arms to another. As time went on and the drinks continued to flow, I noticed that she kept going to one guy in particular. Watching from the outside, I noticed the unspoken pact among the men. This guy had laid claim to her and the others knew to back off. Emily was naive. I wasn't.

The craziest thing was that I wasn't upset. I felt jealous, sure. A little flattered that a younger man would show that kind of attention to my beautiful wife. And pretty fucking turned on. All at the same time.

Nothing ended up happening other than some questionably inappropriate touching on the dance floor. Emily was diligent about moving his hands north, although her resolve seemed to break down toward the end of the evening, particularly during the slower songs. I'll never forget the image of her dancing in his arms, head resting on his shoulder, eyes closed.

That night, we had wild, newlywed sex. I think we were both a little surprised at how turned on we were by the evening. We never talked about what had us both so turned on that night. It was like it never happened, except for the teasing asides Emily would give me when I'd catch her talking to another man—even in innocent, mixed company.

By the time I pulled into my driveway after Bar 88, I was a little sobered up and a lot turned on. Of course, it was neither of these things that my wife noticed when I walked into the bedroom.

"Did you drive home like that?" she asked sharply.

"Like what?" Best defense: play ignorant.

"You're drunk," Emily said, putting her hands on her hips, the dark arches of her eyebrows shooting up.

"And you're sexy..."

She tilted her head to her side, her tussled dark locks spilling across her shoulder. She tried to maintain her stern expression, but her hazel eyes gave her away. We'd been best friends for years and I always knew how to get myself out of trouble. "You think some sweet words'll get you off the hook?"

"They're not just words!" I protested. I checked her out like a teenager. She was ready for bed. Her little boy-shorts and camisole didn't cover much of her body, lean and tight. Since having the kids, she'd always sported a little belly—nothing pronounced, just a softness around the edges she didn't have when she was younger. For the first time, I realized that that softness was gone, along with the little pooch. How long ago had she lost that?

I felt my cock rise, seeing her as Ray did: as a woman he wanted to bed. I reached out and touched her neck, running my thumb along the smooth skin of her jaw. She nuzzled into my touch.

I stepped even closer, forcing her to look at me with those luminous eyes. When we kissed, I imagined Ray kissing her. My cock grew even harder. I felt her breasts compress between us, felt the exposed flesh between her small top and even smaller bottoms. I pushed my tongue past her lips and we kissed like we hadn't in a long, long time.

"The kids in bed?" I asked as we separated.

Emily nodded, looking up at me.

"Come on..."

I couldn't blame Ray for admiring Emily's ass. It was nicely padded with a firm tuck before tapering into her taut thighs. Catching up to her, I slid my hand down the back of her boy-shorts and squeezed.

"Ian." She giggled, rolling her eyes. We kissed again.

I finally let my drunk brain catch up, pawing her tits until I felt her nipples harden under my palms. As she peeled her cami top over her head, I watched her as though it was Ray watching her, and everything felt new. She released her breasts with a healthy wobble. Her nipples were elongated, casting short shadows across the pale swells.

When she shimmied out of her boy-shorts, I guided her to the bed before sinking to my knees. Her lightly freckled skin glowed as I placed kisses along the slopes of her tits, finding each pink nipple and swirling it. Her tips were incredibly sensitive, so I moved on quickly, saving that treat for later.

Squeezing the soft tit-flesh together, I rolled her nubs with my thumbs as my mouth worked lower. Down her stomach. Across her navel. I pushed her onto her back as I kissed across the trimmed wedge of pubic hair she kept above her pussy. I followed it down to her clit, eliciting a shiver and a moan as I passed quickly over it and on to smoother, wetter skin.

I glanced up along her body as I began to work her. She'd propped herself up on her elbows, but her head was lolled back and to the side.

"Oh... yes..."

What Ray wouldn't give to be in my position? To slice his tongue along her slit. To feel her shaved folds along his lips. Drilling a couple fingers deep within her, I twisted and curled in exactly the way I knew she loved.

"Ah! AH!" she cried, remembering to muffle herself at the last second or wake the kids.

I crawled up her body before she could fully recover, pulling off my pants and boxers in the process. Kissing the exposed ivory skin of her neck, I lined myself up and eased into her juicy sex. She was snug but welcoming. She wrapped a hand around my neck as we were united.

Again, I thought of Ray's words, coming at me through the fog of my drunkenness.

Watching her ride me...

That tight body of hers bouncing and covered in sweat...

"Let's turn," I whispered after a few more long and frantic strokes. Emily groaned, but didn't protest beyond that. Riding me was one of her favorite positions.

We reformed at the head of the bed with me reclined on a stack of pillows and Emily easing herself into my lap. I watched her bounce as I collected her tits in my palms and kneaded them gently. Worked her. Got her ready.

"Oh, Ian..." Emily sighed as my lips swallowed her left nipple. I prodded it with the tip of my tongue, feeling her pussy cave around me. She cradled my head against her bosom, using it as leverage to fuck me. I switched nipples, treating the right with the same knowing attention as its twin. Her breath grew shallower. Her sighs took on a reedy, thin sound.

Her voice broke. "Oh... Ian..."

We kissed when she couldn't take it anymore. I slid my hands down her backside, cupping the hard cheeks of her buttocks. I helped her bounce harder. Faster. I could feel her hard nips graze my chest, feel our sweat mix and glide between us. *That tight body of hers bouncing and covered in sweat...*

I attacked her neck, knowing how sensitive she was there. I could taste the salt of her perspiration. Could feel the vibrations of her moans beneath my lips. It spurred me on. I fucked her harder. Faster. She leaned into me, her thighs tightening as she rutted.

She was close. I was close. More sweat collected between our bodies and our skin slithered. She arched back, presenting her wondrous breasts to me. To Ray. To her illicit lover. I saw him holding her, his muscular arms strained. She raked her fingers along her scalp, where the dark locks had begun to clump and cling in their dampness.

"Huhh!" she cried, cumming. "Oh, Ian!"

She climaxed, reaching her oblivion as I smashed through my own. "Cum, Ian! Cum now! Please!"

I clawed down her back. Feeling the dimples above her buttocks. Feeling that ass, wanted by so many. I came, eyes closed, out of breath.

I came with a force that caught me by surprise. That drained me.

The night snuck up on me at last. The booze. The talk. The discoveries. Here's where I should have come clean. Should have talked about these tumultuous emotions inside of me. We could have done the Best Friend thing and worked through it. Instead, I chose to close my eyes and let sleep take me.

I watched her pad naked into the bathroom. I crawled up under the sheets. Sleep was not far behind.

CHAPTER 3

"Oh, Ian! Yes, yes!" I could feel Emily's hands in my hair as she panted beneath me. We'd barely made it into the bedroom before we were all over each other. Lips crashing. Feet stumbling toward the bed. Our hands working at clasps and buttons. I had just enough time to get Emily's jacket off before she had my jeans open and cock out.

"Uh, honey... so good..." She writhed beneath me.

As soon as we'd made it to the bed, all I did was hike up her skirt, pull her thong to the side, and shove inside of her. We were like teenagers, too eager for a proper session.

I ran my hand up from Emily's bare hip out her thigh, which was tight against my torso. Toying with the lacy band at the top of her stockings, I made a mental note to ask her about that later—which was promptly blown away as her body crescendoed against my humping weight.

"Do it, lover... Ian... do... it! Ah!"

Her fingers tightened in my hair. I hammered home, three more times, and released all the pent up energy of the past few weeks. This orgasm was for my wife and the way her luscious body teased me, hard against my own. I collapsed forward, burying my face in the pool of dark hair that gathered on the pillow around her. I drank in the fresh scent of her perfume.

"That was fun," she said when I pulled back to look her in the face. "What got into you?"

"Mmm, maybe I should ask, what got into *you?*"

•••

Earlier that day, I was thinking how no harm had really come of the incident at Bar 88. I'd chatted with a coworker of my wife's, who had the hots for her. I'd received some unnecessary—but welcome—confirmation that I was lucky to have her. And it had been paying off in the bedroom.

Yet one thing in particular began to haunt me. An off-hand comment that Ray had made: *We flirt a little...*Drunk and a little distracted at the time, it hadn't registered beyond the fact that my wife was innocent of any extramarital misdeeds. But now, well, he clearly had a thing for her. Did she have one for him?

When I got home from work, Emily had left a message for me saying that she'd be out at happy hour and not to wait for her for dinner. So played the good husband: had fixed the kids dinner and taken them to the park with the last hours of light.

We were just getting back when I saw the black Mercedes pull up outside the house, just down the block. Emily stepped out, briefcase in hand, still dressed in her work attire, and waved to the departing car. As it passed, I caught sight of the driver, who didn't seem to see me in the dim twilight. It was Ray.

I stumbled a little, steadying myself on the stroller. My daughter, walking next to me, looked up at me before seeing her mother and breaking into a sprint. "Mommy!" she cheered as she dove into Emily's arms.

One child in her arms, she sauntered up to us with a smile and asked, "How's my favorite family?" Our kiss was chaste, although I detected an edge to it. Her breath smelled of alcohol and her cheeks were flushed.

Agitation tightened its angry fist in my gut. *What* had Ray been doing, driving my wife home? Did they flirt? She'd been drinking.

Did they do more?

That last thought didn't elicit the stomach-punching emotion I was expecting. It was more complicated than that. Her blouse was a little more open than it had been when she'd left, one extra button left undone. Ray had said something about that, didn't he?

When she bent forward to set our daughter down, I caught the smooth curve of her breast disappearing into a black, lacy bra. I shifted from one foot to the other and wondered how many others had caught a glimpse of that.

"Who dropped you off, hon?" I asked off-handedly as we made our way back to the house.

"Oh, just a coworker," she said. Did she grow a little red beneath her boozy flush?

"Anyone I know?"

"I'm not sure. I don't think you and Ray have met."

Oh, little did she know...

I put my arm around her shoulder and pulled her close. "He's quite a gentleman, offering to drop you off."

Emily glanced up at me, meeting my eyes for the first time since Ray had been brought up. "You're not jealous, are you?"

"Should I be?" I asked it with a smile, hoping to take the edge off. I felt ragged. I hated to admit it, but I was starting to get aroused.

"To be continued..." she said mysteriously, letting herself into the house.

I watched Emily work efficiently, putting the kids to bed while still dressed in her pencil skirt and slate gray blouse. It was so rare that I got to see her this way. Normally, she went straight to our room and changed into something more comfortable after work. Seeing her the way her coworkers did just added kindling to an already burning bonfire.

Her outfit wasn't overtly sexual. Like I said, it was professional in every sense of the word. But it did a good job hugging her hips, and when she squatted down to grab a diaper from the bin, it stretched nicely across her backside. After Ray, the thought of her coworkers drooling over that sight had been at the forefront of my mind, and here it was, right before my eyes.

"What?" she asked, catching me looking.

I kissed Davy goodnight, grabbed Emily's hand, and nearly yanked her into the bedroom.

•••

"Maybe I should ask what's gotten into *you?*" I said.

I had her pinned beneath me, propped up on my elbows, our faces inches apart. She stared up at me, amused, and I could still smell a little of the alcohol on her breath.

"Your coworker, maybe?"

Emily turned her head away from me, rolling her eyes. "Ian, don't be silly—"

"It is!" I knew my wife. We'd been together far too long for me not to see right through her. And I felt my cock, which had grown soft inside of her, begin to inflate once again. The problem with knowing your wife so well, of course, was that she knew me just as well. As she felt me stir inside her, she studied my face.

"Thinking about me and Ray turns you on, doesn't it?" She didn't seem upset. Just a little shocked.

What could I say? The evidence was against me. "Maybe a little. That's weird, isn't it?"

Instead of answering, Emily kissed me. It started slow and ended fast and hard. And by the end of it, I was hard, too. I wanted to make love to her again, but not like this. Not with our clothes on. I wanted round two to feel less like a quickie. I rolled to the side, shivering as I pulled free of her.

"Do you always look like that when you dress for work?"

She looked over her shoulder at me, her dark hair falling demurely across her eyes. It would have been perfect were it not for her slightly mussed hair.

"You mean like this?" she asked, getting to her feet. She bent at the waist, letting the pencil skirt tighten against her plush ass. I caught a glimpse of the lines of her thong, but more distractingly were the tops of her thigh highs that peeked out through the slit that ran up the back.

I sat up on the edge of the bed and reached out, lowering the zipper of her skirt. "I think it would look better like this," I winked as she wiggled out of it.

The skirt slipped to the floor, and despite the way the shirttails of her blouse fell around her, she was achingly sexy, even without the aid of the thigh highs and heels. But with those...

I thought of the conference rooms at her work. And of how many men must have fantasized about her standing before them as she was now. And of the tiniest possibility that maybe one of them—Ray, perhaps—already had. It made me restless with desire. I brushed my fingertips along her upper thighs, where her skin wasn't covered by stocking. I felt the muscles of her buttocks clench.

She half turned, her fingers coyly tugging at the buttons of her blouse—those that were still fastened. "This is like Bobby's wedding, isn't it?" Had that night been on her mind as much as it had mine? Although we had never discussed it, she clearly had me figured out.

"Yeah. It turned you on, too, didn't it?"

"You know it did, honey." She'd been insatiable that night. "But I was worried about what you thought of me."

"You didn't know? Can't read my mind?"

She finished peeling the blouse off, revealing her padded, lacy bra. The blouse hit the ground. Emily stared at my cock. "I don't think I need to. But do I really want to know what you were thinking that night?"

I had many dirty thoughts that night, all of which involving my wife and the young groomsman. "No, probably not."

Emily reached back and freed her breasts. Still half turned away, I could just see her nipple, swollen and hard in its delicious profile.

"Does that guy who dropped you off ever flirt with you? I mean, you're a beautiful woman."

"A beautiful, *married* woman. But yes, sometimes we flirt. He's just one of those guys. Does it turn you on?"

I pulled my shirt over my head as she turned to me. I didn't miss the way her palms grazed her nipples as she ran her hands down her pale torso.

I pulled my jeans and boxers off all at once, leaving me naked and exposed on the edge of the bed. "Maybe. Is it just flirting?"

"You want to know how serious it is?" Her thumb tugged the edge of her thong down her hip. "Are you asking if it's more than just *harmless* flirting? Does Ray ever push it?"

"Emily..."

"What do you want to know? Do you want to know if he makes passes at me?"

She rolled her thong down her thighs. I glanced across the wealth of femininity before me as she crawled up into my lap. Her nipples were swollen stiff and she was glossy between her thighs. After our quickie, I slid in with ease.

"Does he?" My voice actually cracked like a teenage boy.

"Yes. He tried to kiss me tonight," she whispered. I nearly came again. Probably my earlier orgasm was the only thing that held it at bay. They kissed?

"You knew he wanted you and you let him drive you home?" My fingers found Emily's hips, tightening in their need. Driving her harder.

"Yes." Emily's breath grew short. "I'm a big girl, I can handle myself." She hugged her arms around me, using her hold to start grinding in my lap. "Oh, Ian..."

My wife was as into this as I was. She'd been worked up the minute she was dropped off. "And he kissed you..." I ventured again

"He tried, but I stopped him," she moaned.

I wanted to ask why. I almost said it out loud. She was so fucking sexy: my wife, seen through someone else's eyes. Gone was the cute brunette I'd met so long ago. Replaced was a vixen. "I love you."

"I love you, too, honey." I drew back enough to look her in the eyes. The outpouring of emotion startled me. "I love you so much."

"Show me."

We consumed one another with a passion that bordered on desperate. It felt like the eve of a long business trip, or homecoming after the trip, or when life got too busy to be intimate and we both realized the neglect.

We kissed and pawed, bodies heaving and sliding and dripping with sweat. Entwined, we fed off one another's rise and release. It was pure and primal. Tantric.

"Oh God, oh God!" I cried as I felt myself boil. My fingers sank into her buttocks, helping her drive against me. Helping her finish me. "Uhnnn yes!" I heaved one last time. My lungs collapsed as I climbed my final peak.

My second and final orgasm of the night was for my fantasy. For the forbidden thought of Emily and Ray.

"Yes! Yes! Yes!" Emily's cries were breathy. Shallow. I cringed a little as she fed her fingers through my hair, waiting for the clench that never came. I buried my face between her breasts as we rode out our shared release.

•••

"You know, I was thinking..." We were lounging naked on the bed, all but the thin flat sheet pushed to the floor.

"Yeah? Don't hurt yourself," Emily teased.

In light of what I was about to say, she spoke more truth than she realized. "I think we should meet up for happy hour some time."

"Sure, it would be fun."

I took a breath and decided to push it. "*And* pretend to be strangers."

"Pretend to be strangers?" She giggled. "So you can come in and hit on me?"

I looked away, deflated. At least I had to try. "You think I'm crazy."

Emily surprised me by kissing me softly. "I'm game. When?"

I felt rejuvenated. New life! "How about this Friday after work." I took a deep breath. "I've heard good things about Bar 88."

CHAPTER 4

Friday approached at a crawl, weighed down by feelings of jealousy, anxiety, excitement, and confusion. For Emily, she was no different other than an extra sparkle in her smile as we passed in the house. For me, it was agonizing.

Friday morning just made things worse. I couldn't concentrate at work, despite the fact that actual work needed to be done. I fumbled through the expense reports I had to review, but my mind was on my wife, our happy hour date, and my disastrous plan.

What had begun as an innocent behind-the-scenes glance at what other men thought of my wife had germinated into something unstoppable. I'd received a little taste of something I didn't know that I wanted. Now, I could think of little else. How far would she really go, away from my prying eyes? How far did I want her to go?

Five o'clock rolled around. It was time, and I still wasn't sure if I could do this. The plan was to meet at Bar 88 after work for a couple happy hour drinks. We'd do the roleplay thing that I'd read many other couples do: we'd pretend to be strangers, I'd hit on her, she'd flirt with me, and we'd end up going back to our house where we could pretend to be other people. I'd arranged for the kids to be with my parents. We had all night to be strangers.

But that wasn't the whole of it. The plan was a little more sinister than that—although I convinced myself that it was just an added twist for fun. Bar 88 was where Ray went to shoot pool most days of the week, and my plan was to get "held up at work." I wanted to see what happened.

Emily texted me, telling me that she was going straight from work, but was going to stay a little late to change. I headed over to Bar 88 wearing a New York Yankees baseball cap and a pair of thick, black plastic rimmed glasses. Checking myself out in the rearview mirror, I figured my disguise would hold up. My wife would never guess that I'd wear a Yankees cap, being a die-hard Boston fan, and the Buddy Holly glasses gave me that aging Indy rocker look, rather than "established architect."

I was happy to find that Ray hadn't arrived yet and immediately headed for the dining area on the upper floor. Only a couple of the tables were occupied and I settled in behind a table that gave me a clear view of the bar below. Up here, I could watch without being spotted.

Pulling out my phone, I punched out a text to my wife, reviewing it with a heavy heart as I worked up the courage to send it.

—crisis at work. running late. get a drink. will text with update soon.

"May I get you something, sir?" the pretty brunette server I'd met the other week asked. I shook my head and quickly set the phone face down. Ashamed. "Sure. Um, could I get a Newcastle?"

"Sure thing."

Turning the phone back over, I quickly hit send. If I couldn't deliver this message, then how was I going to be able to take this plan further?

Ray arrived before my beer did. He nodded at the bartender and took up position at a pool table by the back wall. It looked like he'd come straight from work, as he had before. The rolled up sleeves strained around the muscles of his thick arms. Like before, he took to the task of billiard practice very seriously. Everything else was shut out.

He didn't even notice when Emily walked in—although many of the other men certainly did.

As she took a seat at the bar, I almost abandoned my plans and went down to join her. I didn't recognize the chocolate brown dress she wore. Then again, I barely recognized my wife. She reached into her purse to check the message I'd just sent her, and inadvertently treated me with a perfect view down the front of the haltered opening. I didn't see a bra beneath and wondered if she was going without tonight.

She frowned as she read my text. The bartender approached and asked her something. She replied with a nod and soon she had a glass of white wine sitting before her.

I wondered how long this would take, and who would notice the other first. Judging from how focused Ray was on his game, I didn't think it'd be him, although in a weird way, I was pulling for it. I wasn't sure how Emily would react when she realized that her flirtatious co-worker was at the same bar.

In the soft yellow lights of the bar, she was beautiful. Her face glowed from what must have been one hell of a facial. Even her rosy pink lips, heavily glossy, looked like a movie star's.

Emily's eyes swept across the bar, much like mine had last week, taking in the youngish after-work crowd that began to fill it up. For a second, I was worried that she'd spot me as her eyes were drawn up to the shadowy second floor seating area. I drew back and pretended to be consumed with something in my beer.

When I looked back, she was out of her seat and crossing the room, over to where Ray was shooting pool. My heart sped up. Game on.

It was interesting, watching Emily in this atmosphere. She took long, confident strides, sashaying her hips as she approached her co-worker.

When Ray finally looked up from his game, he froze at what he saw. Even all the way across the room, I could see him quickly check out Emily's tight brown dress. *To what do I owe this honor?* I thought I saw him ask.

Emily said something back, her body language friendly without being too flirty, and took up residence on a stool against the wall. She set her phone on the cocktail table beside her as they engaged in a little light banter.

I sent another text, telling her that it was going to be longer than I'd thought, and that maybe we should reschedule the happy hour game. I watched her phone light up beside her. Watched her simply check it without expression. Then turn her attention back to Ray.

Her young coworker missed a shot, turned to her, and held out the pool cue. She hesitated for only a moment. Emily had never shown any interest in pool, so I was a little surprised when she stepped up to the table. My surprise went even further as I watched the way she bent over the pool table, cocking her hips and affording Ray a pretty hefty view of her curvy body.

At one point, in the flimsy guise of an instructor, Ray slipped up behind my wife and corrected her form. She saw right through him, shooting a coy smile over her shoulder as he nestled up against her bent-over frame. My body went hot. As he ran his hand along her bare arm and helped her set her fingers on the felt, the pretense was nearly gone.

I probably could have done something to break this up. Called, maybe, or even just gone down there. But I had no intention of doing anything of the sort. This was as fascinating as watching a lion hunt a gazelle. If things went further, could I handle it?

I was enraptured, watching her flirt and respond. She was the woman I'd met twelve years ago, relaxed and full of energy. She laughed at his jokes. She touched her hair when he spoke.

It was their eyes that gave them away. Their gaze never left one another. They were so into it. When she laughed, she touched her neck and leaned forward, just enough to let him look down her halter top. When Ray emphasized a certain point, he'd touch her gently on the shoulder.

My cock tingled, trying to decide whether to get up or not. In the end, it went up. Way up. I reached for my beer—how many that was, I had no idea—and realized it was empty.

That was when I got the call. The real call. "Ian, we need you. Crisis at the office!"

"What?"

It was one of my colleagues and he sounded uncomfortable. "Well, the plans you turned in today were...um...there were errors in them. We fixed them, but you need to sign off on them." I don't even remember what I did that day! "The clients are going over them first thing tomorrow. You need to get in here."

Oh cruel, cruel irony. When I looked down at the bar, Ray had moved his stool right up next to Emily's. His hand was on her knee as he watched her laugh bawdily, head tossed back, long loose hair cascading.

He reached up with his left hand, dancing it along her cheek before pushing the sweep of her dark bangs over her ear. I knew what was coming next. Knew it, but still didn't believe it.

It happened in slow motion. Emily's laughter petered out. She turned to look at Ray, who was moving his head in. She batted her lashes and bit her lip as Ray cocked his head, lining them up. The hand that had just touched her hair slipped behind her neck, cradling it as he closed the final inches. My wife blinked one last time before closing her eyes. Before accepting.

Ray pulled back just before their lips met. He knew the game. He knew how to play. He watched Emily react to the denial—watches her eyes pop open and her breath catch.

She didn't make him wait long. A beat later, Emily closed the gap, banking her head and covering his mouth with hers.

"Ian, you there?" my coworker squawked down the line.

I jumped, bashing my knee on the table. Their kiss grew harder. More passionate. Even all the way across the room, I could see their jaws working, tongues swarming one anothers' mouths.

"Yeah. Sorry. I'll be there in a few."

"Thanks."

Click.

Ray and Emily broke the kiss in a fit of quiet, secretive laughter, although neither made an attempt to move away from one another.

I watched them for a long minute. Emily's smile was radiant, her head tilted just so as Ray played with the edges of her hair. She was glued to Ray's every word.

All women like that rush of being swept off their feet, you know? Caught up in the moment. Caution to the wind. Ray's words, returning to haunt me.

And then I left. I had to. I'd fucked up at work and right now, that was the immediate problem. Whatever I'd done here would have to wait. Secretly, I was thankful for the distraction.

•••

My fuck-up at work was easy to fix. My staff had done most of the work already by the time I arrived. All I really had to do was seal and stamp it and be on my way, but I didn't want to make the same mistake twice. So I stayed and spent the time going over the plans (while trying not to think about what may be going on between my wife and her coworker).

That took about an hour, during which time I texted my wife, telling her I was trying to wrap work up as soon as possible, legitimately this time. She didn't respond, although she hadn't responded much when I was there, watching. Still, now that I wasn't there watching, it made me really nervous.

As I was almost out the door, my office phone rang.

"Ian?" Emily asked, sounding a little surprised to hear that I answered.

"I'm about to leave, honey." I couldn't hear the sounds of the bar in the background anymore. "Did you go home? I'm really sorry about tonight."

"You... you're at work?"

Something about the way she said it struck fear in my heart. "Didn't you get my text messages?"

There was silence on the other end of the line.

"Did you go home?"

"So you really *did* have to work?" I suddenly realized that it wasn't shock that was clouding her voice. But bitterness.

"I'm on my way out the door now."

"Well, in that case, don't wait up. We're not ready to go home."

"What—?" The line was dead before I finished my sentence.

I was a cartoon villain who'd wandered into an obvious trap: the floor had dropped out from under me, yet I was too stubborn to fall with it. What held me up? Couldn't have been the same thing that was holding other less savory things up, was it?

I said goodbye to my coworkers, apologizing once again to them—I was apologizing too much lately. My drive home was dark and lonely, a funeral procession of one. I thought about the night. I thought about watching Emily; what it was like to watch her be with someone else. Someone who wasn't me.

I couldn't deny the stirring it caused—some goddamned funeral this was turning out to be—and yet I knew that no matter what kind of expectations I had for tonight, this wasn't one of them.

I swung by the bar, but despite wasting fifteen minutes searching the drunken crowd, I couldn't find either of them. My heart cringed. This was not the way I'd planned it at all.

CHAPTER 5

"Welcome home, Ian."

I was half-way toward the stairs when I heard her voice. Emily's, low and sleepy, coming out of the living room. It was so unexpected that it nearly knocked me off my feet. I blinked as I saw her sitting there, curled on against the padded arm of our sofa, her silky pink robe draped around her.

Details started filling in. The lights were on in what should have been an empty house. Emily was no longer in the sexy trappings I'd spied her in earlier. Her make-up was washed away. Her hair was back in her standard-issue ponytail. This woman hadn't just gotten home. She'd been home a while. So...

"You're home," I said, confused. I walked into the living room and sat down next to her. This felt like a dream that had just taken a disorienting swerve. "You...the phone...I thought you were still out..."

"Out with some stranger? Is that what you wanted? Was that really your game?" She still hadn't moved from her spot on the armrest.

She sounded mad. This wasn't good. "I'm sorry I got hung up at work."

I felt arousal lick along the back of my neck despite the situation.

"I thought you were watching me," she said.

The lick took on a new feeling. She knew? She'd spotted me watching through my disguise?

She went on. "I thought that was your game."

My throat tried and failed to make saliva. I felt exposed. Ashamed. Shit! "I'm sorry."

Emily looked sad. At last, she uncoiled herself from the sofa and wrapped her arms around my neck. She was hot in my lap and I could smell the tint of booze on her breath, making things fuzzy around the edges. "You have no idea..."

She kissed me on the neck, soft enough that it almost tickled.

"What happened tonight?" I asked as I thought about the kiss she'd shared with Ray. Did she know I was watching? Did she think I'd been watching all evening long?

"Not right now," she whispered, trailing kisses along my jaw. Our eyes met as she reached my lips. She rolled her forehead against mine. It was clammy. "Later."

And then we kissed, ragged and feverish.

I felt the buzz of disaster in that kiss. It was lurking there, just moments away, yet I couldn't reach it. Couldn't rush to it. I was forced to wait and felt impatient because of it.

Channeling that, I yanked the robe open and off her shoulders and tore my mouth away from hers. At first I thought she was naked, her succulent breasts filling my humming brain. As I took in the brown garter belt and matching thong, I realized this is what she must have had beneath her dress tonight. So she hadn't completely removed evidence of the evening...

We struggled with my clothes as our mouths crashed. I was hard as Emily peeled me out of my boxer-briefs. She stroked me as we kissed, firm jerking motions that would have hurt if I wasn't so turned on.

I shoved her back onto the couch. Passion overwhelmed me. I was going to remind her who her husband was. Spreading her legs, I ripped the thong off. Emily yelped. I gave her no time, lunging forward and sinking into her.

"Uhh, yess..." She groaned. She was as moist as I was hard, and we both knew the reasons were less than pure.

With my brain painting everything I raw red, I finally found the guts to ask the question I'd been wanting to ask all night long. It emerged like a snarl: "Are you going to tell me about tonight?"

Emily's earlier hesitation was gone, washed away in the tide of lust. "I...I thought you were watching...set me up..."

"Watching what?" My cock flexed inside of her.

"I...I didn't mean..." I saw her fear like fireworks reflecting against a lake. Fear mixed with excitement and hunger.

"Didn't mean what?" I demanded, ramming my hips into her.

"I...I kissed him...uh...Ray was there...didn't know...thought you were there...watching..."

This time, I didn't feel shame at being caught. I was too focused on her confession. I wanted to drive it out of her. Needed to. Fuck, *she* needed me to!

"I...I saw...some bad disguise..." she stammered as I thrust swift and hard between her legs. "I thought...oh, Ian...I thought you wanted..."

"Wanted what?" The buzz was back.

"Wanted to see me kiss Ray!" she cried, tensing beneath my weight.

Her eyes began to withdraw as an orgasm took her. I fucked her harder, determined to keep her with me. The couch scraped along the floor, shifting as I put my entire body into my jamming hips. "You liked it, didn't you?"

"Ian..." Her eyes were looking wet.

So here's where I should have said I actually *was* watching. Where I got her off the hook. Where I told her that the evening was, in fact, a game, and that she'd played it marvelously. But she was as guilty as I was in this crazy night—if not more. I felt fire in my veins.

"Whether I was there or not, you wanted it." I groped her buttocks hard, spreading my fingers so wide the webs of my hands began to hurt. Her hips danced as she felt me raise her up on my girth and pull her back down. "Something got you excited..."

"Ian..." A hesitated warning.

"Whether I was there or not was moot. You still did it. And you still liked it." I tightened one hand on her ass, drawing her lush body up into me. Forcing her to help me fuck her.

"Ian..." The hesitation eroded away to something deeper. Something buried.

"Tell me! Tell me you liked it!" I wanted to hear it. I wanted her to confess. To be verbally masochistic. "When he was behind you, touching you. When he brushed your cheek and kissed you..."

Recognition lit my wife's light eyes. They flared up. She blinked away her tears, raked her fingernails down my back, and thrust up into me.

"Uhn... yes! Yes, baby! I liked it when Ray kissed me." Gasoline on a camp fire. "I loved it when he touched me!" Flaring up. "I wanted him!" She screamed it all and I was screaming with her.

"EMMM!"

I felt her shiver and shudder around my cock. I quickly joined her, erupting deep and hot. We clung to one another long after the orgasm, our bodies fighting to catch our breaths as our minds caught up with the revelations.

"So you were there..." Emily said at last, easing up off of my softening cock.

The shame was back, that feeling of my hand being caught in the cookie jar. "I was, but then I got called away by a real work emergency. How long did you stay?"

"You're such an asshole. How could you set me up like that?" Her words were harsher than her tone.

"I'm sorry, I don't know why I did it. I just wanted to see..."

"Wanted to see what?"

"I don't know exactly. I just wanted to see you..."

"Wanted to see me flirt with other men. That's what really turns you on, isn't it?"

There it was, something I'd been struggling to come to grips with since, well, since Bobby's wedding, and my wife went and stated it so simply.

"Yes," I admitted, almost more for myself than for her. And I felt terrible for it.

"Is that all you wanted to see?"

When I'd embarked on this plan, I'd never thought it would lead me here. But then that was the problem: I didn't know where it would lead. I didn't think that far ahead. "I don't know, Emily. I swear I don't know."

"Honey, shhh, it's okay. I'm mad you set me up, but I did have a good time. I just wish you'd come to me."

What, wait? "You would have said yes?"

"To flirting? Probably. If Ray wasn't there, I don't know what I would have done."

So she didn't know the full extent of the setup. Good, I planned on her never knowing about that.

"Christ, I can't believe I did that with a coworker." She buried her face against my shoulder as I felt myself begin to revive.

"But you did do it. You kissed him and you liked it, and it wasn't just because I was watching, was it?"

She looked away from me, sighing. When she looked back, she looked more confident. "Yes, I liked it, but I wouldn't have done it if you weren't there." Something flickered across her face. Guilt? She went on. "I liked knowing you were watching. It made me hot to know you were seeing me like that."

"So how long did you stay? What happened after I left?" I wanted to know, but didn't. Again, that verbal masochism.

"When I saw that you weren't there, I panicked. I thought you might have been pissed or something. So I got out of the bar as fast as I could."

"And called me when you got home." She nodded. I could see the whole night unfolding for her. Felt her panic.

"Yes. I almost passed out when you answered the phone. You were my safety net while I was out there. I thought you wanted to play a game and it was so exciting."

"But then you thought I was never there?"

"And that's why you're an asshole. I went through hell."

I nodded. I knew I was in trouble, but then, I also always knew how to get myself out. "But you enjoyed it."

"God, Ian!" she said, punching my chest. She tried to push me off her, but I held firm.

"I enjoyed it, too," I admitted. "It was the hottest thing I've ever seen."

She felt me begin to stir against her thigh. "I know you did. But I don't understand why."

I didn't have an answer to her question, but knew I had to come up with one. "I can't really explain it. I like seeing you enjoy yourself." That seemed mildly truthful.

She saw through the dodge, her eyes flashing with anger. "Enjoy myself?"

Shit. Back peddling. "Okay, not just enjoy yourself. I like seeing you sexy. I like seeing other men want you."

"And if they kiss me? If they touch me?"

"I don't know. That turns me on, too, crazy as it is. None of this makes sense. I know I'm nuts..."

"It's a little crazy," she agreed.

"I mean, tonight was harmless, wasn't it? It was just a kiss." I watched her, wondering if more had happened. I didn't know if I could ask. She didn't take the bait.

The air felt heavy. I watched her chest heave with each labored breath. "This is dangerous, Ian. It could get out of hand. What if he didn't want the just kiss? What if he walked me back to my car?"

I already began to rise at what she was implying, even if I knew she had to be fucking with me. Maybe because of it? She pushed me off her and straddled me, circling my cock in her little hand. She ran it across her smooth lips, still slippery from earlier.

"What if it was more than kissing? Are you okay with that, too?" I jerked in her hand. "What if I let him touch me?"

"You wouldn't..."

"I think you'd like that." She taunted me, all the while using my cock like it was a dildo. Who was this woman? I wondered as she stroked her clitoris with the ridge of my dickhead, tickling the crown in her closely cropped landing strip. She squeezed me. "I think you'd want to see it," she said, like that was evidence.

"That thing doesn't speak for me." I looked down at my fully erect cock in Emily's swiftly stroking hand. God, but it sure as hell *felt* for me at times like this.

"It really turns you on, doesn't it? You thinking about Ray groping me in the dark car, sliding his hand under my dress?"

She crawled out of my lap and onto the floor, getting onto her hands and knees. I was so sorely tempted. The swollen perfection of her lips shined between her thighs. But I wanted to hear more. "He loved my garter belt," she whispered. "He was playing with it all night."

I couldn't believe it. Emily reached between her legs and ran her fingers across her pussy. She was so wet. "Ray pulled on my garters... uhnnn..." The fingers disappeared between those lips. "He pulled them while he fucked me..."

That was all I needed to hear. I followed swiftly, sliding into her from behind as she braced herself on the coffee table. "Nggh! He...he fucked me...just like that...yesss, Ian...sooo go—ood..."

I watched her tight body, splayed out before me, the chocolate brown lace of her belt framing her round ass. This was the image her lover would have seen, if she'd been telling the truth. I knew she was lying. What I didn't know was whether this was my fantasy, or hers.

"Oh, Emily!"

I grabbed the lace garters like reins and pulled. Emily responded. "Fuck me! Fuck me!" Fantasy or not, she was feeling something.

I didn't cum with her second orgasm—not so close on the heels of my first—but I did come close. The illicit vision she was filling my imagination with made sure of that. The queasy sensation of jealousy and unease was still there, lurking beneath the surface. It was the danger that excited me.

"It didn't happen. Ray didn't fuck me." She was trying to console me, when that was not what I wanted. I flipped her over and entered her in a smotheringly comfortable missionary style.

"Did you want to?" I asked, my eyes boring into my wife's.

"Maybe? I don't know." This woman was killing me!

That was what I wanted to hear, and yet... "Really?"

"I just don't know. It was so hot, kissing him with you watching, but I don't know if I could."

I moved faster inside her. Harder. Felt her skin swelter against mine. Felt the softness of her lace at my hips. "Getting swept away by some handsome stranger turns you on, doesn't it?"

"Yes, baby, it does. Oh, Ian, do it. Do it, honey…"

Her fingers traced patterns on my lower back and across my rocking hips. She was right, this was dangerous. A path littered with signs warning of pitfalls and hazards. I ignored them all, blindly stumbling forward and into the murky dark.

"Do you want to see him again?"

"Do you want me to?" I was close. Emily encouraged me, grabbing my butt and pulling me into her.

"Yes. I'm sorry, but I do," I confessed.

"Don't be sorry, I want to play, too." Was she saying it because she knew it's what I wanted to hear? "I want you to see me with Ray."

"Ahhh…do it! Do it, Emily!" I cried, cumming deep and hard into her. My energy vacated. I fell forward, a quivering mass of confused flesh. Nothing more was said. Had I just given her unspoken permission to keep playing this game?

Could it be called permission if I didn't understand it myself?

CHAPTER 6

I couldn't sleep the next morning, despite all of last night's excitement. I laid in bed, filled with nervous energy as I waited for the sun to rise. I'd pushed things too far. In the sober morning hours, I realized my mistake. How could this be a game if even I didn't know the rules?

When it felt like a decent hour, I crept out of bed and headed downstairs. The backs of my eyes hurt from lack of sleep and I needed coffee, badly. I was on auto-pilot, pulling the French press out, boiling the water, steeping the grounds. The middle of summer was hot in these parts, but things were still cool in the morning. I took my coffee and sat out back.

I thought of Emily and the life we had. It was a good life. Really good. We had two healthy, intelligent children. We had a stable working life and a nice little home, out in the far suburbs. When I thought of where I'd be when I was in my early 40s, this was it.

So why had I gone and done what I'd done? Why risk throwing all of that away?

The answer wasn't an easy one. I couldn't directly answer Emily last night, and I couldn't answer myself now. I didn't think it was specifically some cuckold fantasy I wanted to experience. I didn't want to be humiliated. I didn't want my face rubbed in it. I just liked the idea that other men were attracted to her. And I liked that she liked it, too.

I sat on our back porch, trying to work it all out and getting nowhere.

Our lot bordered a wooded stretch of land. We loved that it felt less planned than most sub-divisions around here. Somewhere down there was even a bubbling brook that Davy would love to play in when he was a little older.

It was peaceful out here. The calm before the storm?

I heard the door slide open behind me but didn't turn. Emily was up.

"Ian, honey, why didn't you wake me?" She kissed me on the top of my head and took a seat beside me.

"You looked like you needed the rest." She did. She'd looked so beautiful.

"That's true enough," she agreed softly. "Last night was…something."

My heart contracted. I kept staring out at those woods, thinking that maybe, just maybe, if I didn't look at her, this would all go away.

"It was." My hand tensed around the coffee mug. I wondered if I could shatter it with enough pressure.

"You know we need to talk about last night."

I felt hot. Trapped. Fuck, fuck, fuck. "I know."

"And it can't wait. Can you look at me, Ian?"

This was Emily, alright. She paid the bills on time, never was late for an appointment, and when it came to problems, she met them head on. I just wished I wasn't the one causing all the problems.

"Honey," I began, seeing some of her own anxiety in her face. Suddenly, it became easy to talk. "I'm so sorry. I don't know what I was thinking setting you up like that. I just thought it might be fun to play that way because, you know, of the way we felt at Bobby's wedding."

"Ian, babe, it's okay, calm down." She took my hand and squeezed it tightly. That felt good. A connection. "I don't know that it was a bad idea. I just wish you'd told me that's what you wanted to do."

I looked down. "Would you have done it?"

"I think so."

I blinked. Really? It would have been that easy?

"I wasn't sure." I felt even worse. Now I was completely the villain. "I knew you would like it but I didn't know if you would *do* it, so I thought if I just put you there…"

"That was a shitty thing to do, Ian. And it wouldn't have worked. If I hadn't spotted you there I would have left."

I licked my lips. Emily was right, but still…that wasn't the way it had played out.

"But you didn't."

"No, I didn't."

"And you went over to see Ray." The setup had worked. It had been a gamble. Hell, the whole fucking night had been a gamble. And now…

"I wanted to teach you a lesson. It was like Fate—Ray being there, I mean."

I did everything I could to not react. "And if he hadn't been there?"

Emily shook her head. "I have no idea. Probably nothing. But I'd already had a couple glasses of wine, and the memory of how turned on you got the other night when he'd made a pass at me was still fresh on my mind…"

I kept waiting for her to put it together. To question the coincidence. I acted before she could. "I think it was perfect. It was so hot, watching you two flirt. He was so into you."

"He kissed me!"

"That was awesome. Do you hate me?"

"Of course not. I love you, Ian. I love you as much as I ever did. What happened last night wasn't…normal, but that's between us. We can do anything we like. We're two adults and whatever we choose to do in our marriage is for us to decide."

I squeezed Emily's hand. She always did this. Was always full of surprises. When all I could see was darkness, my wife came along with a light and helped me see that it wasn't so bad. And the thing she showed me now happened to be quite a turn on.

"Did you like kissing Ray?" I asked.

She looked at me meaningfully. "I'm going to be honest with you, Ian. I always will be, so don't ask me anything you really don't want the answer to."

I took a deep breath, filing that away. "Okay."

"Yes, I enjoyed kissing Ray. He's handsome and I know he wants me and that makes me feel sexy."

"How long have you known he wanted you?"

"I never thought about it before this week. We've always flirted, but I never thought it meant anything. He knows I'm married."

"Guys don't care about that so much, Emily. If they want to fuck you and you give them an opening, they'll go for it."

Emily laughed. "It's like that *When Harry Met Sally* thing. I guess men and women can't really be friends if there's an attraction. But I don't know if Ray wants to…fuck me." Emily stumbled over those last words. That only got me hotter.

"He does. Trust me." The words tumbled out, nearly betraying my illicit knowledge.

"How could you possibly know that?"

"I, uh, just know the type and I saw how he was looking at you.

He wanted you."

Emily appeared to buy it. She seemed more focused on the implications than how I knew. "And that turns you on?"

"It does." I shared some of my insight from earlier. "Seeing how other guys want you really turns me on. Watching you flirting with Ray in that sexy dress last night was incredible, Emily. It was like I was seeing you for the first time."

"And you weren't jealous at all?"

"I guess a tiny bit, but no, not really." Not quite true, but also not quite a lie. The jealousy was part of the excitement, I was beginning to realize. Part of the arousal. But if Emily thought I was getting jealous, I was afraid she'd end this whole game before it began. "I was too into it to be jealous." Another test; I added, "And it was hot because I knew you liked it, too."

She blushed, a pinkish glow sweeping up her graceful neck to harbor in her cheeks. I glanced down, noticed that her nipples were pushing hard through her thin tank top. There was no denying it; I wasn't the only one getting off on this.

She spoke slowly, picking her words with care. "I feel like I got the better end of the stick, though. I got to have all the fun. I don't think I could handle watching you with another woman."

"I don't want another woman. I only want you, Emily. It's always been you."

"And I just want you…" She let the sentence dangle.

I knew there was more. "But?"

"There's no but, really. It's just that yes, an attractive younger guy coming onto makes me feel sexy and with you there, looking on, I felt like I had permission to maybe play a little bit. But that doesn't mean I'm not happy with you."

"I know." And I did. It was liberating.

"And I could never do that without you there. You're my safety net. I know things won't go too far if you're there. I mean, it was hotter *because* you were there. I don't want us to turn into one of those couples where we're just the mom and the dad and you don't see me as a woman anymore. It was like I could show you how sexy I am and even show you I can still be dirty and hot. And since I know it turns you on, that just makes it so much better."

God, who was this woman that had replaced my wife? Had she been there all along, waiting for a Ray to bring it out of her?

"Did you stop when you realized I wasn't there?" Another unthinking question, raised more by my cock than by my brain.

Emily looked away, hesitating. "Not right away." If there was a scale between 1 and 10 of hardness, and my dick would have broken that scale now. "I mean, I knew I should, but Ray was insistent. When I went outside to get away he went with me. He was there when we spoke on the phone and then he drove me out to my car."

"Did he kiss you goodnight?"

"Yes. I mean, after everything else that didn't seem so bad."

Everything else?

I don't think I even blinked. I don't think I had a chance.

"What was everything else?"

If I'd have remembered my coffee, clutched forgotten in my hands, I would have raised it to my lips, just to wet a parched throat. But all I could think of was Emily's words: *everything else.*

She looked bashful. Red. She bit her lip and shook her head, her eyes nearly as wide as my own.

"I didn't have sex with him, you have to know that, okay? Do you really want to know everything?"

Did he grope her? Did he get his hands inside her dress? Under it? Did she...holy shit, did she blow him? I looked up at her. She was nervous. More nervous than ever, when she started this enlightening conversation. There would be more opportunities, I realized. And this time, maybe I'd be able to see whatever *everything else* was.

"No, not this time," I said.

"This time?" she asked, shocked at my implication that there would be more. I felt the balance of power once again returning to my favor.

"How did you leave things with Ray?" A plan was hatching again. She answered, but I wasn't really listening anymore, other than to hear that she hadn't killed it between the two of them. This time, though, I knew I needed to include her in it. She'd told me to, hadn't she? "I…I think we should play again. I think you should hook up with Ray."

"What? Ian, I have to work with him! I don't want to be the office slut."

"Listen, hear me out. I like that it's Ray *because* you work with him. It makes it more dangerous, and that makes it more exciting."

"Right, but you don't have to deal with the fallout. I do."

"Didn't you mention he's leaving soon?"

"Yeah, they've transferred him to the office in Philadelphia. He's only got two more weeks here, but that's not the point. You're right, it *is* dangerous."

"But because he's leaving it's not *so* dangerous. Think about, Emily. It could just be like a little goodbye fling and then he's gone and it's over. Once he leaves, there's nothing to worry about."

Once I latched onto something like this, it was hard to let go.

"Philly's only a couple hours by train," she pointed out. I waved that excuse aside for what it was: an excuse. She was buying into this. I almost had her. Just needed to prove it. She asked, "You really want this, don't you?"

"I do. Come on, Emily. Last night was amazing. I know you felt it, too. Where's the harm in playing around for a couple weeks if it's going to make us feel like that?"

"Why does it have to be Ray?" Her last, weak defense. She'd all but waved the white flag.

"I told you. I know you like him. I saw how much you liked teasing him, but this time it won't just be a tease."

"You just want me to ask him on a date?"

"Just let him know you had a good time last night. Trust me, he'll do the rest."

"So then I go out with him and what happens? You know you have to be there, right? I want you watching me."

"I guess you guys go out and see what happens, that's all. I know it will be great."

"And if something does happen? How much should happen, Ian? What if he tries to get me alone?"

"Go out to his car or something. I can sneak up and keep an eye on you." Just thinking about it had me practically salivating.

"You didn't answer me. How far should I go?" This was where I had to tread lightly. Anything too crazy and I'd spook her, no matter how open the new Emily was. If she was doing this for me—which I got the impression she was—then getting her to agree to fuck him was probably going to end in a lot of egg on my face. So I was vague.

"Just go with it. Do whatever feels natural."

"Ian…"

"I trust you, okay? We're in this together. Do you have Ray's number?" I had her. Now, I just needed to do something to lock her in.

"It's in my phone."

"Go get it."

I watched her stand and disappear back into the house. Her hair was still a little wet from her shower and, as the norm, she'd tied it back into a long ponytail that flicked between her shoulder blades. Coupled with a tight gray tank top and black boy-shorts, she looked youthful.

She handed me her phone and I immediately navigated to Ray's number. I was relieved to see that she'd had no previous text conversations with him, even as I began one of my own.

–great time last night. can't wait to see you monday

"What did you do?" Emily asked, grabbing the phone from me. Her eyes lit up when she saw the message I'd written. "Ian!"

Before she could get mad, I grabbed her and kissed her. Hard. We'd been talking way too long and I was too horny to keep it up any more. I yanked her tank top over her head and palmed her breasts, feeling their weight in the crisp morning air. We'd never fucked out here and I started wondering why. Unless someone was hiding in the woods or had set a ladder up against the high privacy fences on either side, no one would ever see.

Hear us... now that was a different matter.

"Ian…"

"We're going to play, aren't we?" It was more a suggestion than a question, delivered with kisses down her neck.

"Yesss…" Music to my ears.

Emily's phone chirped. I grabbed it before she had a chance to see, reading the message. "Ray says he can't stop thinking about last night. Says you can talk at the gym. Hey, you never mentioned you work out with him."

"I don't," she said, trying to get the phone back. "He goes to my gym, but we don't workout together. Gimme that!"

Another bolt of inspiration washed over me as I began typing once again. She reached for the phone, but her efforts were half-hearted. She liked this little tease, even as I got her into trouble with her coworker. I held the phone behind me, kissing her when she tried to snatch it away.

I pushed her back onto the lounger and blew her another kiss. Still reaching out, she cocked her head and put on a wry smile that said, *You're five seconds from being murdered.*

I swept the phone around and snapped a picture with it. Priceless. I got a good look at it just before I hit send. While it didn't show her nipples, it was pretty easy to tell that she had nothing on where the photo was cropped. And with her hand outstretched, it looked like she was taking it herself. Perfect for the accompanying text:

–here's something to really think about!

Finally, she lunged at me, jumping out of the lounger and grabbing the phone for good. "I can't believe you just sent him a topless picture of me! You are out of your mind!"

I didn't correct her. She could figure the truth out on her own.

"And you're loving every second of it." I turned her against the railing, bent her forward, and rolled her boy-shorts down her legs. With a hand on the small of her back, holding her there, I dropped my own shorts, fisted my cock, and sank into her.

"Admit it, you like Ray having that picture?" I grunted, holding her shoulders for support as I fucked her.

"Ian...I...yesss..." She did. She fucking did!

"You can't wait to go out with him again..."

"Yesss...Ian...fuck me! I can't wait to kiss him while you watch us, baby!" Her words inflamed me. We didn't do this. We didn't talk while we had sex. Now, it seemed so natural.

"Uhhnnn..."

"He's gonna kiss meeee...and touch meeee...and...ohhhh...I'm gonnaa touch himm..."

"Touch his dick…"

"Yes…"

"Suck it…"

"Yes…oh yes…baby… You like that? You want me see me suck his cock?"

"Uhn…yes…"

Neither of us could speak after that. I grabbed Emily's tits in my hands, squeezing them, pulling her nipples as I felt her climax build. Build and crash. And I fucked her right through it—

fucked her silly, thinking that maybe, just maybe, it'll be Ray behind her. Splitting her pussy open. Filling her!

I groaned for the whole neighborhood to hear. I pushed her hard against the railing and pounded without mercy.

And at last, I was sated. And this time, I felt good. Free.

"I love you, honey. I love you so much."

"I love you too, Emily."

CHAPTER 7

"Say it again, baby," I huffed, plowing my stiff fingertips along Emily's shimmering back. She rode me, facing away, her moans muffled so that we didn't wake the kids.

"Yes... I want to... fuck, baby... want to hook—hook—ah! Hook-up with Ray..."

"Are you thinking about him now?"

"Yes!" she cried, her voice piercing through the night. We both caught our breaths, dampening our grunts as we listened for the kids. They didn't stir.

"You're thinking about him fucking you?"

"Oh, Ian, cum," Emily pleaded, refusing to answer. My balls tightened and I came, unable to pursue the questioning. I wondered if she was. I still felt the inkling that she was doing all of this to humor me, despite the evidence stacking up against that.

We'd been like this all weekend. I don't know how many times she'd gotten off, and I was definitely at record setting levels. We teased and played around the subject of her date with Ray, fucking every chance we could get. The kids occupied our days, so that left us the evenings and we weren't getting much sleep.

We'd monitored Ray's text conversation, but the only thing he texted back was a single word: *WOW!*

This guy knew when to play it cool. That should have struck cold fear into my heart, but it only kept it racing faster.

Monday morning, I watched Emily get ready for work. I didn't normally do that, but today was special. Today was the first official day of our unnamed game and I didn't want to miss a detail.

Emily knew her audience. Played to it. I watched her emerge from the shower, watched the way she dried her water-beaded skin. She had a sexy ritual to her morning activities, one that I'd really started taking for granted. In the bathroom, she slathered herself in body butter until it was rubbed in, leaving her pale skin with a delightful sheen. A different lotion went on her freckled face, and a different still was worked into the smooth skin around her trimmed pubic wedge.

She slipped into a little black satin thong and paraded about doing seemingly mundane things. I knew she was teasing me, but it was great. Was she paying special attention to her make up this morning? Did she brush her long chestnut brown hair out a few more times? She certainly took her time rolling her stockings up her legs, right before my eyes.

"I love those," I commented as she eased the expensive silk along her shapely thighs.

"I know you do."

"But I thought you always hated them."

"That's because garter belts are a pain in the butt, but these stay up on their own and they make me feel sexy." She snapped the lacy top against her thigh for emphasis and we shared a soft, sensual kiss. "I know you're looking at my ass." She laughed as she walked back to the bathroom.

Her instincts were true. I couldn't take my eyes off the way the satin plunged between her round ass cheeks.

Her work outfit was a little more risqué than I was used to, as well. I hadn't seen the light gray suit in a while. We jokingly referred to it as her *Melrose Place* suit because of how short the skirt was. It was short enough to show off her legs, and I was hard thinking of what Ray would think of that.

"Let me know how lunch goes," I said as we kissed at the front door.

"I'll text you," she winked, catching me eyeing her cleavage down the front of her jacket. She'd put on a lace-trimmed camisole blouse, which was typical, but the push-up bra that matched her thong was padded enough that suddenly she had a tempting line of décolletage. And that wasn't even from bending over.

•••

Monday was the day I reserved for site visits to the projects I was responsible for. It meant a lot of driving around, a lot of inspections in hard hats, and usually some trouble shooting. Other than driving between sites, the visits required my full attention.

I was thankful for the escape. Otherwise, I'd be thinking about what Ray and Emily were doing all day. As it was, the short commutes were killer. What were they doing for lunch? Were they working out together? I knew it was improbable, but my mind even conjured a fantasy that involved the gym's shower room, some soap, and not much else.

Around two o'clock, I finally got a text message. My phone buzzed while I was being walked through the nearly completed atrium of a downtown site. The foreman was chattering away with an associate and I risked a peek. Had to. The words on the screen floored me.

–worked out with ray. date tomorrow night. he kissed me.

Bang, bang, bang. Just like that. It wasn't sex in the shower room; it was better because it was real. I licked my lips, glanced at my co-workers, and texted her back a quick message.

−excellent. details tonight. can't wait..

Fucking A, the rest of the day was going to be hard to get through. Her text burned itself on the backs of my retina. Every time I closed my eyes, I saw those words. They'd worked out, after all. I thought of the outfits Emily owned to work out. I thought of the skin-tight black leggings and her equally tight sports tops. I thought of the way her sweat collected between her freckled breasts. Ray wouldn't be able to keep his eyes off her.

And apparently, he hadn't been able to keep his lips off her, either. They'd kissed again! Things were moving fast. So fast that...

"Date tomorrow night!" I cackled the words allowed as I navigated my way to my third and final visit of the afternoon. I knew Ray wouldn't let me down. He knew his time was limited and he seemed intent on moving fast. It was too bad the date wasn't tonight, but at least this would let us get set.

•••

That evening, I asked Natalie to stay a little longer as Emily and I got "settled in." She said it was no problem, although the sparkle in her eye suggested the nanny knew that something was up between us. What kind of a couple did she think we were?

As soon as I heard Emily's car pull up, I was at the door, waiting for her to walk in. "Welcome home, honey." I beamed, kissing her warmly on the lips before the kids had a chance to swarm.

"Hi, honey." My wife was all smiles. She was out of her jacket, looking so tempting in that satin camisole top. I wondered if Ray had seen her like that. I hoped he did.

"You have a good day at work?"

"Mmm hmm." She winked. I glanced at her lips, wondering how many times she'd had to reapply the gloss. I followed her upstairs as Natalie herded the kids outside, giving us some time. Emily glanced back at me with a smirk, but said nothing.

We were fucking practically before the door was closed. It wasn't lovemaking. It was fucking, raw and hard. I released all the pent up sexual frustration I'd been carrying around all day, and apparently Emily had some steam to let off, too. Nothing was said until we'd cum together and lay in a tangle of sweaty limbs, still half clothed for work.

"Thanks, I needed that," she said, flopping onto her back.

"So you have a date?" As much as I wanted to hear about the workout and the kiss, I cut right to the chase. We didn't have much time before we needed to be mom and dad again.

"Someone's eager," Emily laughed.

I stared up at the ceiling, watching the fan spin. "You weren't complaining a couple minutes ago."

"Fair enough."

"Well, Ray was eager, too. He wants to cook me dinner."

I swallowed hard, trying to digest that. That was a lot more intimate than I'd thought we'd agreed on. I felt Emily shift next to me, studying my face. "We compromised on Bar 88 instead. I just couldn't figure out a way to sneak you into his apartment." She giggled.

I was more relieved than disappointed, although there *was* disappointment. If she'd gone back to his place, there was no doubt what would have happened. "Were you tempted at all?"

"Ian, honey, no. I told you, I can't do this without you. This is *our* game, not mine. And certainly not Ray's."

I believed her intentions. I believed that's what she believed. But she also admitted to kissing Ray while I wasn't there. I left it alone.

It was Emily who eventually brought it up, later that night when the kids were in bed and we could take our time with each other. "You haven't said anything about me kissing Ray..."

The lights were out and I couldn't see her above me beyond a collection of smooth shadows, but I could hear her hesitation. This had been on her mind all evening long. It had been on mine, too, along with the flirting they must have done at the gym. I did want details, but I also didn't want to push her. To scare her off.

"Do you want to talk about it?"

"I think we should."

"I'm not upset, if you're worried about that. I mean, it's not like I haven't seen that before."

She was quiet as she rode me. Had I touched a nerve? Had more happened that she didn't tell me about? "How slippery is this slope, Ian?"

"Did it feel natural, to kiss him?" I asked. Just saying that aloud sent a jolt through me.

"Yes," she whispered.

"Then stop overthinking it. I'll let you know if I think things have gone too far, okay? Nothing more was said, although we did reach a mutual orgasm there in the dark.

CHAPTER 8

I was *nervous*. Fuck, was I nervous. Every nerve ending buzzed, from the tips of my toes to each follicle of hair, and no matter how deep I breathed, I couldn't draw enough air.

As I walked into Bar 88, things only got worse. Or better? Or something. Fuck, who knows?

I spotted Emily at the bar, alone at the moment. Our eyes met and we shared a brief nod before taking our stations: me upstairs once again, my wife crossing the bar to the pool tables where Ray was already shooting. My heart fluttered. Pretty soon, things would be irreversible.

Emily blended better with the crowd tonight. I'd tried to get her to vamp it up again as she'd gotten ready, but she was right, the jean skirt and purple cardigan gave her that co-ed-look that Bar 88 favored. I remember her complaining about the shortness of the skirt in the past, but in this bunch, it was pretty modest.

She sauntered up to Ray, who was turned away, surveying the pool table, and I realized it wasn't just the clothes that helped her fit in here. It was her confidence. She'd always had it, just in small doses. Here, you could practically see it radiating off her. She flipped her loose, dark hair over a shoulder, ran her hand up Ray's back, and accepted him into her arms.

He turned, wrapped an arm around her slim waist, and pulled her close. They kissed. Just like that. No flirtatious words. No giggles or sighs. The kiss was their greeting and I nearly fell out of the balcony leaning forward to watch. Things certainly had progressed! Had they only just kissed the day before? Had something happened today? Before I could conjure more unsettling questions, Emily leaned away when it looked like Ray wanted more.

Her coworker let her go, giving her a once over before complimenting her on her outfit. I'd thought she looked cute in a sexy way, but I wondered if Ray only saw the sexy. The cardigan really did mold to her torso, and I'd never seen her wear it without a tank top beneath. That, combined with the liquid-padded push-up bra I'd spotted on the bed earlier—a gift from me, once upon a time—really helped complete the Playboy version of what a co-ed should look like.

Ray had bought her a glass of wine already and I had to smirk. The guy had come here with the single-minded intent to get laid. I wondered if I was okay with that. When he backed Emily against the cocktail round and kissed her again, I figured that at least part of me was. His hands took more liberties, sweeping across her ass. We'd never been like that before. Never so free in public. I always thought it was Emily's reluctance, but maybe it was mine...

I went through a pint and a half as I watched their first game of pool. Watched them flirt and cavort. Emily did as much brushing and teasing as Ray did, bending and stretching to maximize the curves of her body. It took me about half the game to realize she was doing it as much for me as for her...date.

That word. *Date.* This was a date as sure as anything, but she wasn't out with just one man. As she glanced up at me for the third time with her kohl-lined eyes and deep red lipstick, I realized she'd done her make-up not just for Ray, but for me as well. She'd put on that outfit for both of us. She'd slid into those high, wedge-heeled sandals so that both her men could drool over what it did to her legs.

It left me queasy and heady and aroused all at once. My heart wasn't going to slow down until it exploded. I loved that she was into this game. And I loved the flipside to my most recent observation: she was doing this as much for Ray as she was for me.

After the first game, Ray disappeared and Emily looked up at me. She was smiling. She was enjoying herself. I didn't trust myself to move, to give her a thumb's up. To do anything but sit and stare. Ray returned with a tray that held not only a refill on their drinks, but a couple shot glasses of clear liquid and two lime wedges sitting beside them. Tequila shots. The last time Emily had done a tequila shot—over five years ago—we'd been so worked up that we didn't even make it home in time to fuck. We had to pull over into a park and fuck in the backseat.

The shallow breathing was back. The plan had felt so simple when conceived: a couple walks into a bar, separately; one flirts with the guys while the other observes. I quickly realized that nothing was that simple. I wasn't the only man on this date hoping to get into Emily's panties tonight.

And yet, I couldn't stop myself from watching. And watch I did. Ray shook salt onto his wrist as Emily picked up the clear glass. She looked him in the eye, ran the flat of her tongue suggestively across his bare skin, and slammed the shot back. When he lifted the lime wedge to her mouth, she made sure to dance her tongue across his fingertips before biting into the tart meat of the fruit.

I'd been stationed at the upstairs bar, where it met the railing, but now I couldn't help myself. I'd moved to the banister so I could watch the scene, hoping my dark-rimmed glasses were enough of a disguise if Ray looked over.

I wasn't the only one, though. Ten feet down was another guy taking a breather. He nodded at me as we went back to people watching. Emily and Ray were just two in a sea of humanity, but I wondered if this guy was watching them, too.

Emily had her head tipped to one side, her hair raked over her shoulder to bare the white skin of her neck. She'd wet it and applied the salt there. Jesus Christ! Ray's hands went around her waist as he played the part of vampire-seducer, sucking on her neck. The damsel swooned before he pulled away long enough to down his shot and eat his lime. And then they were kissing again. Hard and passionate. I caught a flash of tongue as they shifted their heads and worked the kiss some more.

"That guy right there is one lucky motherfucker," my fellow people-watcher commented as he went back to the bar. I didn't say anything. I just nodded.

The man was right. Ray was lucky. Was he going to *get* lucky? Not here, of course. As long as they were in the bar, my wife's virtue was safe...ish. Ray would want to go somewhere else. What then? Would I be able to follow? What if he took her back to his place? What then?

I ran my hands through my hair as the next game was played, this time with even more flirtation. More touching and posing and playing. They must have made some kind of bet because when it ended, after a little reluctance, Emily reached up and popped the top button of her cardigan.

I couldn't believe it. The purple, clingy material was already low enough. With one undone like that, her freckled breasts were on full display. Playboy co-ed indeed! At certain angles, I could even see the lacy trim of her ivory bra. I'd seen her in that thing before.

They flirted a little more before starting up the next game. I wondered what was said. What bets were made. I wished I could have heard. I watched as Emily shot with refocused energy. She was no longer putting on a show for me and Ray—she was trying to win. Yet with her cardigan like it was, the show was better than ever. The two of us weren't the only ones to take notice, either. Every time she leaned over to take a shot, eyes swung in her direction. They all wanted her. They were all imagining what those twin orbs would look like naked. It was thrilling, not just for me, I realized, but for Emily. Unfortunately, it also threw her off her game.

Ray was all over her. Always touching some part of her body. His fingers would linger on her arm, or touch her hand, and rub the small of her back. Until about halfway through the match, he was a gentleman about it—gentleman in the romantic lover sense. At some point, though, the touches became more. His hand would run across her ass as she bent for a shot. Or he'd nuzzle the crook of her neck when she missed.

I had not imagined how far our game could *really* go. I mean, I hoped that I could see Emily like I'd never seen her before—see my wife stretch her wings and take flight. They'd kissed. They'd flirted like mad. And now they probably wanted more. Ray certainly did.

We were exploring the outermost reaches of my expectations. Was I prepared for it to go beyond them?

I wondered if Emily was. She certainly reciprocated Ray's affection, although not quite so obviously. She didn't leave his side when he took his shots, and at some point, she started rewarding him with each sunk ball with a kiss. I wondered if even she realized the bond that was beginning to build between them. The patrons around them sure as hell did. The kisses intensified until Ray finally sunk the eight ball and pulled her into a long, swarming kiss of victory. Emily actually looked weak in the knees, and swayed a little as she made her way to the restrooms. When I was sure that Ray wasn't following, I took the back stairs down to meet her. I caught her just before she pushed into the ladies' room.

She was flushed. Even in the dark corridor at the back of the bar, I could see that.

"Ian," she breathed, falling into my arms. "Honey, I don't have much time." I slipped my hands down her forearms and held her at her elbows. Her skin was burning beneath the thin material of the cardigan. "Ray wants to take me someplace, but I don't know where."

I felt my body sizzle. Goosebumps formed on my wife's arms. Here we were, leaving the known territory of this fantasy. This game.

"Do it," I said, drawing her close. Goddamn, I wanted her. I had half a mind to pull her into the bathroom and fuck her in a stall. Now that would be a first. She must have felt my intentions because she pushed me away before our kiss really got started.

"Are you sure? I could just tell him I have to get home."

Last chance. The final opportunity to end the game before any more lines were crossed. But on the other hand, this may be one of the last opportunities for us to explore this side of our relationship. Ray was safe. The week after next, he'd be gone. Out of our lives forever.

"Do it, Em. I'll follow you guys. Just try to make sure I can see you guys." Christ, make sure, I thought. From this point on, we were operating without a net.

"What if he wants to…?"

"I trust you. Just do what comes naturally."

I knew she hated that cop-out answer, but it was the best I could do. When she walked out of this bar with Ray, I was as much in the dark to my desires as she was. All I knew is that right now, I wanted her to leave with him. Emily gave me a last peck on the cheek and disappeared into the ladies room.

I leaned against the wall and tried to take hold of the whirlwind I was caught up in. I spent the next five minutes trying and failing. Emily emerged, her hair and make-up touched up. I couldn't help myself as I gave her a once over and nodded. There was nothing trampy about her look—I just wasn't used to her with that much make-up on, or that much cleavage.

"Good luck," I whispered with a soft kiss on her lips. Emily blushed and nodded, strutting back out to the bar. Me, I disappeared into the bathroom, wondering how I was going to pee with this hard-on. I was just softening enough to get the proper angle when Ray swept into the bathroom and took up a position beside me.

"Hey, buddy!" He said, recognizing me despite my disguise. "Nice glasses."

My first instinct was to lie. To deny that I know him. To say, *Have we met?* My second was to run. Maybe not even zip up. Just turn and bolt for the door without a word, my erection forging the way.

"Thanks," I said instead, glancing at him out of the corner of my eye. "I didn't see you here!"

"Didn't see you, either. Funny I should run into you, actually. You know that chick we were talking about last time?" I was thankful that I met him in the stall because I had male bathroom etiquette as an excuse not to look him in the eye.

"Yeah..."

"Well, she's here. With me, I mean. You should meet her."

I stuffed myself back into my jeans and zipped up. "Really? So you went after her?"

"Oh yeah, man. I owe you a drink for that one.

I scrambled to breathe. "Yeah?"

"You were right. With two weeks left and nothing to lose, I decided to go for it. I was right, too. She's definitely got a wild side under there."

I wanted to curl up under the sink. Instead, I just nodded like an idiot. "Awesome, man."

"I think I've gotten lazy. So many girls are so easy these days, but sometimes, it's the ones that are hard to get that're the best."

"So you've *gotten* her?"

"Not yet. Soon though. Very soon." He winked. "Come on, meet her. You'll see what all the fuss is about."

"I shouldn't. I need to get back to my friends. They're probably wondering where I am already." Knowing that they were leaving, I added riskily, "Maybe later?"

Ray shook his head, "We're actually about to take off."

"Back to your place?" I can't believe I fucking asked that. My heart was in my mouth.

Ray grinned. "Haven't been able to convince her to go there, yet." *Yet...* "But some place more private." He slapped me on the back. "Have a good evening!"

He threw open the bathroom door with more force than was needed. It swung around and crashed against the wall. And then he was gone.

•••

Tailing Ray and Emily proved very difficult. I almost lost them a couple times as they tore through the night in the younger man's glossy black Merc. I panicked once as I turned the corner onto an empty road. On one side, the row of upscale boutiques were closed and dark, the parking lot empty. On the other was a large condo complex where not all of the garden style apartments had turned in for the night. My heart leaped in my chest. Had Ray taken her back to his place, after all? How was I going to watch now...?

Not knowing what else to do, I pulled into the gated complex and began to drive slowly through the small, car-choked streets, hoping to spot the flashy ride. I began to give up hope and visions of Emily getting pounded by Ray's solid body started haunting me. It was a little arousing to think about, but more than anything, I felt regret. And hurt. I felt left out and realized that I needed to be there, just as much as Emily needed me to be there. Then I spotted an empty parking lot in the back of the grounds, and on the far side, Ray's car.

I shut off my lights as I pulled into the lot with them and watched the darkened cab of the car for a good minute to make sure no one occupied it. I sucked in air through my nostrils, tasting the sweet smell of relief on the back of my throat. The dull hurt faded and I pulled into a space in the corner of the lot, as far from the other car as possible. As I slipped out of my Toyota Camry and shut the door quietly, my adrenaline surged. This was happening.

I surveyed the dense copse of trees past the empty Mercedes and saw the glittering blue light at last. A pool. He'd brought her to his complex's pool. He must live in the condos. It was a simple deduction, but I felt like a super spy making it, and even more of one as I crept into the trees.

The adrenaline brought everything to life, colorizing what was once a black and white world. I could smell the sweetly chemical odor of chlorinated water, strong as it mixed with the crisper, cooler scents of a late summer night. The wavering lights of the pool were wiped like restless spirits, anxious to escape the dark leaves. And at its heart, I heard voices. The low grumble of a man's and the softer lilt of a woman's. My woman's. She was giggling.

The pool wasn't large, surrounded by a concrete patio and adorned with a single diving board. I could just see them...embracing? Standing close? I was so focused on them that I nearly ran into the black, wrought-iron fence that apparently surrounded the place.

Cursing under my breath, I slinked through the trees, hoping to get a better view on the opposite side. Their voices carried across the water before dying in the shrubs around me, although my pulse was beating so loudly in my ears that I couldn't make out a damned thing. Settling into a particularly dense growth of brush, I hunkered down and finally got my first unobstructed view of Ray and Emily.

Well, first of just Ray. He'd just finished stripping down to a pair of black boxer-briefs, stretching his tall, gym-hardened body as my wife looked on.

My chest tightened. This was all happening. This was real. I could fantasize and hypothesize and wonder all I wanted, but here was my wife, alone with a man wearing nothing but his underwear. All kinds of lines were being crossed, and there I was, trampled beneath those stomping, eager feet.

I could certainly see what women saw in Ray; he had one of those upper bodies that you saw on the cover of Men's Health—hairless muscled perfection, right down to the six-pack abs. I just never realized that my wife was into that look. Yet when I looked at her, there was no doubt that she was licking her lips as she surveyed her Adonis.

In fact, her eyes were glued to him as he walked to the edge of the pool and lowered himself in. The submerged lights danced across the patio floor. He dipped beneath the water, breaking the surface and facing my wife. They stared at one another for a long moment.

My heart thumped heavy in my chest as I watched. She glanced in the direction of the trees and, unwittingly, right at me. I gave her the thumbs-up, although I knew she couldn't see that. She seemed on the verge of leaving when finally, she took a deep breath and reached for the top-most button of her sweater.

If I'd been hopeful that Emily would end the game, that hope died as she undid her sweater, lingering on each button with a coy twist. Her confidence grew as she stripped, along with her comfort. And while mine remained a buzzing mess, this was her moment. Her transformation. When she pulled the purple cashmere thing open to the night air, she did so with a flourish. She spun it once before tossing it onto a cushionless lounger. Her jean skirt soon joined it with a quick shimmy.

"Damn." Ray whistled as she stalked over to the pool's edge, still wearing her wedged heels. "I knew you were hot, but I had no idea."

Another man was looking at my wife in nothing but sexy lingerie. My beating heart sounded like a fucking tidal wave in my ears. The world seemed to slide sideways. I caught myself as I swooned, squeezed my eyes shut, and took a deep breath.

Get it under control. This is happening. You fucking wanted this.

When I opened my eyes, no more than a couple seconds had passed. Emily was still standing there, her hip cocked a little as she glanced down at Ray through the valley of her cleavage. The ivory lace of her bra and snug panties made her look expensive—sexy in a sophisticated way.

Ray paddled close to her, slicking his dark hair across his scalp.

"Don't shout. It's a little cold," he warned as she began to lower herself into the water. Her face tightened as her toes kissed the edge of the water. Ray scooped her up in his large hands, holding her on either side of her bare ribcage. Emily gasped at the skin on skin connection as he pulled her into the water.

I echoed her gasp. The bar was gone with their clothes. They'd left innocence with the pool cues and green felt. Now they were adults, frolicking together half-naked in the gleam of an empty pool. And I was as weightless as they actually were.

He pushed off the wall, buoying them out into the center of the illuminated pool.

"I can swim on my own, you know," I heard Emily say. Her words helped me refocus. I blinked away my doubts, holding it at bay for now.

Emily pushed away and floated up onto her back, her wet curves rising like the smoothed landscape of a glacier. Ray held her feet to keep her from floating away, and watched her as intently as I did.

Ray floated her toward her, sliding his hands up her legs and across her body, which was glistening wet with water. Her legs parted around his body as he worked his hands across the ripe swells of her breasts, pulling the cups down across her nipples. She sank back into the water. Into his arms. I could just see her legs as they wrapped around his waist. And then they were kissing.

They whispered to each other, but I couldn't hear what they were saying. Sweet nothings, perhaps? Emily was certainly smiling, even when she exclaimed, "Ray!"

The younger man took advantage, pulling her into a deep kiss as his fingers went for the clasp of her bra.

I gasped. Emily stopped him. Ray didn't pause for a beat. He kissed along her jaw and down her slender neck. Emily tilted her head to the side, her dark, wet hair draping across her shoulder as he worked her jugular.

He kissed her lower, strategically drifting them to the pool's edge. She held his broad shoulders and squeezed with her thighs... grinding into him? Could it be? His lips found her breasts—found her swollen nipples over the lowered top of her bra.

Emily's moan pushed the last pockets of air from my lungs. I gasped for air as the scene continued to play out.

Ray drew her moan out. I saw his teeth closed around the tip of her nipple before the two of them drifted to the pool's edge and out of sight.

All I could see were the wet tops of their bodies. Emily shut her eyes, lounging back on the concrete lip, and moaned as Ray worked wonders to her sensitive nips.

She's into this, my mind screamed. She wasn't doing this just for me. This was for the two of us. I reached down and adjusted my cock, which was riding a painful angle down my thighs, and prayed for Ray to push it.

Ray finally did. He kissed along her flat tummy, lifting her back to the surface of the water. My heart skipped a beat as Emily's voice drifted to my ears.

"What are...?"

She looked uncertain, glancing for the tree line—this time in the opposite direction where I was crouched. She was afraid. Uncertain that things would go too far for me.

"Ray, I don't know..."

Her protest was weak and short lived. He slipped her legs over his shoulders and began to nuzzle along her thighs. My throat was dry. I rubbed my cock through my jeans.

When Ray nuzzled her mound through the panties, Emily jumped, but didn't push him away. Instead, she groaned, her head lolling back, her eyes closed tightly. Ray held her ass as he teased her, grinding his lips and face against her pussy until she was right at the edge.

"Ray...Ray...mmm, Ray..."

Everything felt out-of-body. That should have been me there, prodding my tongue along Emily's panty-clad pussy. But I was crouched fifteen feet away, rubbing myself as another man did the honors. This was no dream, no matter how much it felt like one.

She had to be close. With all the kissing and teasing, with the way he'd sucked on her nipples and kissed along her thighs, she had to be really fucking close.

And then he backed up.

"Ugh! Ray, what...?"

He let her stew just long enough to catch her breath and moan a protest. "Ray, don't stop—"

He attacked her panty-clad mons. Her cry skipped across the pool's surface as she clutched the concrete edge.

He pulled her panties to the side and she protested for one brief moment.

"Nononono—"

He drove two fingers into what must have been a slippery pussy. She cried as he twisted into her, his mouth going back to work on her clit, protected just enough by her panties that he could get rough with it—that he could torture the knot of nerves without overloading her.

"Ray! Yes, Ray! RAYRAY!"

I'd only ever heard her cry *Ian* like that, her throat straining under the firm press of pleasure. This was my wife cumming at the touch of another man.

If there was remorse, she didn't show it. That only made me harder.

Ray lowered her back into the water and they were all over each other again, lips and tongues crashing as they rubbed their near naked bodies against one another. Emily's right hand disappeared beneath the surface. It only took me a moment to realize what was happening. Ray's own hand emerged, his sodden briefs in his hand. As he flopped it on the concrete skirt, their bodies returned to one another.

Jesus Christ, were they...were they fucking? I watched Emily's hands clutch the fit young man's shoulders. She rocked her body, tossing her head back. Ray trailed butterfly kisses down her proffered neck before she met his lips again in a volcanic embrace.

My jaw hung open. They were fucking! I thought I'd imagined this moment before, but it had always come with a little more warning. They'd be fully naked. There'd be the careful line-up, the splayed thighs, the opening thrust. I forced my hand off my cock before I came. Had to shut my eyes and look away as the vision of them almost sent me over the edge regardless.

And then they climbed out of the pool and I realized they hadn't been fucking at all. Emily's ivory boy-shorts were still on, clinging to her moist and swollen lips. I could see the dark stripe of her pubic hair through the translucent lace. Her bra was still pulled down, the padded cups displaying her bared tits like a Playboy Centerfold.

Ray rose out of the pool like in a Calvin Klein commercial, water washing down his muscular nudity. His erection curved bluntly before him, catching in the dancing lights of the pool.

Emily kissed him without hesitation, their casual embrace twisting my gut more than her recent orgasm. Their lips smacked as she pulled back, wet and painful to hear. Whispering something with a giggle, she boldly reached between them and wrapped her hand around his erection.

I gasped. Just like that, without warning. I became disembodied again. I was with her, but I wasn't. And when she lowered herself onto the rim of a lounger, I *really* wasn't.

My breath caught. I knew what was coming next, but refused to believe. Every muscle in my body tightened. Everything stopped. The world receded to the muted pounding of my slowed heart in my ears. She leaned forward, stroked Ray's thick cock once in her hand, and ran her tongue across it. She looked up into his eyes, studying him as she curled that silky tongue across his swollen cockhead and slithered down the underside.

I groaned in frustration as her damp hair fell forward, blocking my view. My obstruction lasted only a moment. Ray kindly pushed her clumped locks over her ear just in time for me to watch her take Ray into her mouth.

"Em…"

My wife's pale lips stretched around his veiny girth. She took three-quarters, working it slowly, in and out, in and out. I could practically feel her mouth around my own cock—feel the familiar way she swirled her tongue along its crown, or the way she jacked her hand in time with each bob.

But it wasn't me she was sucking off. It wasn't my cock tickling the back of her throat. She was blowing another man, and I was getting off on it.

Emily looked up at him from there on the lounger, their eyes meeting and holding one another. Jealousy rose to the surface. I was suddenly very much aware that I was a voyeur—an onlooker literally on the other side of the fence.

My wife wrapped her fingers around his balls with her free hand. This was her finishing move, the thing that always got me to pop. Ray responded differently. His fingers seized in her damp locks, taking control of her mouth. Fucking her face, even as she sucked harder, her mouth corkscrewing along his length.

"Emily, fuck… Em… so good…"

I watched her. Watched *my Emily*. Her eyes remained focused on his, an intense study of lust and indulgence. I may have pushed her to this point, but there was no doubt that in this moment, with another man's cock pistoning in and out of her mouth, she was into it.

Even as his eyes creased at the edges and his orgasm raced forward, their gaze never broke.

It was a moment that I wasn't part of.

"I'm gonna cum, baby... fuck, I'm cumming..."

My thoughts thinned out and my senses dulled. The world folded in on itself.

Emily didn't stop the blowjob. She didn't slow down even as Ray's balls began to empty. Watching Emily's cheeks cave around another man's pulsating cock is an image that will stay with me forever, and will probably always bring that heady mixture of eroticism and wrongness. This was an Emily that I hadn't seen in forever—that I barely saw even before Ray—and she was so fucking sexy.

Across the concrete patio at the edge of the pool's wavering light, my wife desperately fought to swallow all of another man's cum. She almost did it, but his virility proved too much at the end. Her throat muscles flexed, even as Ray's pearly white cum dribbled down her chin.

"Holy shit! Why did we wait to do this until now?" Ray exclaimed as Emily scooped up the excess cum before it could drip onto her bra-clad tits. Still holding his softening member in her fingers, she got the rest of his juice off his balls with a delightful sweep of her tongue.

"Because we shouldn't be doing this at all. I'm a married woman, remember?" Emily looked down at her wedding band, then off into the woods.

"Right," Ray grinned.

"Speaking of which, I really need to get out of here." She asked him to turn as she peeled off her wet bra, releasing her beautiful tits to the night air at last. Ray stole a glance before she was able to pull on her cardigan, but Emily didn't turn away. She also left half the buttons undone, leaving more than an appropriate amount of cleavage on display. The skirt went on before the panties came off, but did she flash him?

Her hand slid into his as they made their way up the path and out of my view. Stuffing my own cock back into my pants, I pulled out my phone and texted her a quick: *see you at home.*

I snuck into the house, where Natalie was asleep on the sofa. I let her lie for the moment, creeping into the garage to wait for my wife.

The fear struck, there in the dark. As the minutes ticked by, I wondered what was taking so long. I didn't even need to close my eyes to imagine the two sharing kisses against the car door, their hands wandering. Ray's apartment was *right there.* Had he convinced Emily to go back to his place, after all?

Craziest of all, it wasn't the fear of *what* they were doing that was coiling around my chest and squeezing; it was that they were doing it and I couldn't see. That I didn't *know* about it. And this fantasy of mine—this obsession—needed to know.

The garage door opened before that fear coalesced into action. Checking my watch, I saw Emily was only a few minutes behind me. When she got out of the car, she had an odd look in her eyes. A little challenging, a little amused. The cardigan barely covered the decent halves of her breasts and her nipples were hard points through the purple cashmere.

"Ian, I…" Words failed her.

They failed us both.

"Emily," was all I could say before I was all over her. I tore open her sweater as she attacked my pants, freeing an erection that was stronger and harder than ever. I bent her against the storage rack, hiked up her skirt, and swiftly penetrated her.

"I saw you. I saw it all," I grunted as I filled her. Not an hour ago, another man had two fingers in her sodden pussy. Not an hour ago, she was bobbing swiftly along his cock. "I watched you suck his dick."

"You liked it, didn't you? You liked me swallowing his cum…"

God, her words inflamed me. I grew harder. Stroked faster.

"Uhnnn.... Em.... yesss..."

She pushed her hips back into me as she moaned. "He made me cum... so hard! God, fuck me, Ian!"

"Emm..."

The rack beat shrill and loud against the cinderblock wall of our garage. I didn't give a fuck. I took my wife like she needed to be taken: hard and fast. This was animal passion. This had been building for far too fucking long.

At last, when we were spent and holding one anther lovingly, she looked up at me and whispered, "You know I love you, don't you? I love you so much. Whatever happens with Ray doesn't change that."

"I know, Emily." I did. I had no doubt about that. Not for a moment. No matter how passions grew when she was with Ray, she was there in the first place because of me, and she would never have gone out with him alone if it weren't. "I've never loved you more than right now."

We kissed again and I grinned. "I think we woke the nanny..."

CHAPTER 9

"So I was wondering..."

"Oh dear." I could hear the trepidation in my wife's voice down the phone line. I could practically see her rub her brow.

"It's not bad, actually, I promise." I'd been springing so many surprises on her these past few days that I understood where she was coming from. "I was thinking about maybe meeting you for drinks after work." She sighed and I pressed on before she got the wrong impression. "Not like last night. Or last Friday. I was just thinking let's...let's put this game on hold. For a night. I just want to go out with you—as your *husband*—and have a good time."

"So you're really going to show up? Not text me about having to *stay late at work*?" she asked suspiciously.

"I really will be there."

"And you won't hang out at the bar, pretending to be a stranger?"

"Nope. In fact, let's go to a restaurant where there's not even a bar."

"Ooh, classy."

"Meet you at Don Lorenzo's at 7?"

•••

The Italian restaurant was in our neighborhood—and more importantly, nowhere near Bar 88. I went straight from work and arrived before our reservation.

Emily must have gone home to change, because she wasn't wearing the pin-striped pant-suit she'd gone to work in. Crossing the room, clutch purse bouncing at her side, I don't think I remembered my wife ever looking this confident. Her hair even fluttered around her shoulders like the slow-motion shot of a movie star walking onto a set.

She looked pleased to see me there, touching my face when she joined me in the waiting area as though she needed to feel me to believe me. Her face was filled with relief.

"Yes, it's me. I'm here."

"Thank you," she whispered, kissing me softly on the lips. I skimmed my palms along my wife's cowl-necked tunic blouse, resisting the sudden urge to grab her hard and pull her close.

"You look good." I stood back to look her over. She'd belted the white blouse and wore leggings with her tall, black boots. "I should have gone home to change, too."

"Nah, I like you the way you are." She touched my tie, running her fingers up the silk and straightening it the knot at my neck. "Is our table ready?"

We were seated, put in our orders—including a bottle of Cabernet—and now came time to talk. Last night sprang to mind, of course; watching my wife fool around with another man in the ethereal lights of the submerged pool lamps. My pants tightened.

"So..." Emily said, her voice throaty.

"So..."

Her bangs were pinned straight back and a couple loose strands framed her flushed face. She cast her eyes downward. I reached out and touched her hand, which was playing nervously with the still-empty wine glass. "My day was killer!"

I launched into a mundane recount of office politics and tedious tasks, bracing a little for an annoyed wife. But it didn't come. Instead, what came was worse. She withdrew a little. She felt more distant.

I mean, on paper, everything felt great. It was like before Ray, when our conversations didn't surround dangerous flirtations with other men. I knew I needed the respite—if only for tonight—and by the time our food arrived, Emily seemed okay with it, too. The only time things did stray close to the game was when we talked about her work and the new responsibilities she'd be getting when Ray left.

"More client-to-client interaction, more staff to manage, more responsibility..." She wasn't complaining—Emily was a very hard worker and welcomed the new challenges—she just didn't like being taken advantage of.

"More money?" I ventured.

"They're consolidating the jobs into one for budgetary reasons. I seriously doubt I'll get a raise." She sipped her wine as she looked away in thought. "I thought the company was transferring Ray to Philly to help manage the office there, which is true. But there's a little more." It was strange, hearing her talk about Ray in a non-sexual way. Her voice was warm. Affectionate. "He told me he asked for it because he's not sure how much longer TNK will be around and wanted to be closer to his family, in case he was suddenly unemployed." I felt an uncomfortable twinge of...something. Since meeting him at the bar, I'd been slowly reducing Ray to something abstract: a toy for my wife to play with. Emily was humanizing him again.

"Jesus. If anyone's job wasn't safe, I figured it was the architects."

"Government contractor jobs are in danger in the new administration. I mean, I get it, bring the work back to government workers, but...just doesn't seem fair when it affects us." I reached across the table and took her hand into mine. She looked up at me, clearly worried.

"We'll be okay."

"We will..." I felt the *but* in her voice, waited—it didn't come. Was she worried about Ray? The twinge was there again, and this time, I knew what it was. Jealousy. I banished the thought.

Emily emptied her glass. "I guess when Ray leaves, I'll really have to go back to being an adult."

•••

I paid Natalie as my wife slipped upstairs to check on the sleeping kids, and then joined Emily at the door. "They're so peaceful," Emily whispered as we watched our son's slow breathing shadow. "Say goodnight to Jenny. I'll meet you in the bedroom." I heard the promise in her voice. I knew what that meant.

Emily was sitting on the edge of the bed, legs crossed, smiling at something on her phone. She tapped out a reply to whatever it was and her phone lit up with an immediate response that made her laugh out loud.

"Keeping secrets from me?" I teased as I closed the door behind me and loosened my tie.

"I don't think this one's a secret," she said, wagging the phone at me before putting it away. "Jealous?"

I yanked my tie from my neck and tossed it onto the bed. I was a little jealous, but even more, I was turned on. As I watched her sitting there on the bed, looking up at me all innocently, I again thought about how stunning she was.

I sat next to her and just stared. She didn't say anything, batting her lashes and looking at me coyly as I reached out and touched her face. I brushed my thumb across her high cheekbone, dusted with freckles, before moving down her jaw into the nape of her neck. Our first kiss was as soft as her skin and as restrained as our entire night. I could feel her passion ramp up as rapidly as my own, and yet I kept the kiss lazy and slow.

Our lips separated and I rolled my forehead along Emily's. "I love you, honey."

When we kissed again, the restraint was gone. My nostrils flared as Emily's tongue dove into my mouth.

We undressed each other. I worked her belt open as she struggled with the buttons of my shirt.

"Here, let me." I slid across her fingers as I popped open the rest of my buttons. Emily scooted up the bed, rolling onto her back, and pried her boots off. I twisted around and watched her undress as I did the same.

She shimmied out of her black leggings next, keeping her lingerie a secret beneath the long, cowled blouse. I stood so I could get my trousers and boxers off, stretching my shoulders back in what felt like a masculine show for her. Emily grinned as she looked up and down my body and the erect cock that was soon in my hand. Then she pulled her top off, finally giving me a glimpse.

I groaned at the sight of the lacy purple bra. "That's new."

"I ordered a few new things." She winked, carefully arranging the low-rise matching thong around her hips. "You like?"

I dragged my hand up her legs as I crawled on top of her. The purple lace was deceptively soft as the tip of my cock brushed along it. "Did you get it for me, or..." I felt Emily stiffen and immediately knew it was the wrong thing to say. "Or for you?" I finished lamely

Emily's focus shifted between my eyes as she studied me, chin tucked, from her reclined position on the bed. Reaching up, she grabbed the back of my head and yanked me down into a hard kiss.

No more talk, she was saying. She'd given me one pass and I was pretty sure I wouldn't be given another.

I broke the kiss and whispered, "You're so sexy..." I nuzzled into her neck and up the soft lobe of her ear.

Her fingers were wild in my hair. "Oh, Ian..." she moaned as I ground my length against the gusset of her panties. I could feel her moisture and heat there. Feel her need. Is this what Ray had felt last night in the pool? Or had he pushed that barrier aside, if only for a moment?

I jerked a little at the thought and forced my mind back to the present. I *had* to force it back; tonight was about the two of us, not the game. Not Ray. Looking down at her, her dark hair unraveling from the clips that had held it back, I repeated myself. "Emily, baby, you're so fucking sexy."

"Show me, darling." She sighed, running a hand down my back and across my clenched buttocks. My mouth enveloped hers again, humid and feverish. I released her tits from the bra and licked her nipples. Emily gasped above me, stifling her near orgasm.

"Show me more," she breathed. I dragged her thong down her legs and lined my cock up against the swollen lips of her pussy. I stroked the length of it with the ridge of my manhood, teasing before pushing into her.

We shivered in unison. I swelled inside of her, her words rising to the top of my brain like fizz off a soda: *show me, show me...* And I did. I planted my arms on either side of her as she wrapped her legs around my waist.

"God, Em... you feel... sooo... good..." I groaned. I felt the heels of her feet dig into my lower back and sank down onto my elbows. The pillowy crush of her breasts spurred me on and I savored the drag of her nipples. Our sweat pooled and mixed as skin slipped along skin.

Try as I might, I couldn't keep last night out of my thoughts. It crept in with each thrust and moan. The way she'd looked up at Ray as sucked on his cock. The way she'd twisted and cried as he'd eaten her out. The mixed emotions of the night returned as well: the confusing cocktail of jealousy, betrayal, and excitement. Another man, fingering my fucking wife, and I only got harder.

I kissed her hard one last time before pushing up, first onto my hands, then all the way up to a kneel. Her face contorted as she did her best to stay quiet. Her fingers couldn't stay off her breasts, though, and as I watched her twist and rub her nipples, I nearly lost it. Her eyes were closed. What was she thinking? Was she thinking about him?

"I'm close... are you?" I asked, surprised by the scratchiness in my throat.

"Yes, baby...close...so close..."

I fucked her with long, hard strokes, jerking her hips up into me with each downward thrust. Her right hand joined our union, sliding down her landing strip and right along her swollen button. Three heavy flicks and she was writhing. I'd held my own orgasm at bay long enough. Without slowing down, I released it, filling her in an overflow of stifled moans.

I collapsed next to her, sated at last. "I don't think I've ever been so sweaty after sex," Emily laughed, running her hand through her damp hair.

"I'm sapped."

"Good night, Ian. I love you." She rolled over and I met her in a soft kiss.

"I love you, too." And with that, life went back to the game.

CHAPTER 10

If anything, the great sex just got better. It wasn't always furious and frantic, but the unspoken game was its own presence in the bedroom and neither of us would deny it was on our minds. We just never brought it up.

I had to admit, I knew I was on borrowed time. Ray would be gone soon and everything would go back to normal. Until then, life felt like a fuse, sizzling along to some grand explosion. But I just couldn't help myself, and Emily wasn't giving me any reason to stop.

I was in the middle of a conference call with an out-of-state client and bored out of my mind when my mobile phone rumbled to life on my desk. Answering it would have been highly unprofessional, but since I was only a nominal part of this project (and not quite sure why I was even in this call), I checked.

Answer your phone, read the text. From Emily. It began buzzing again before I even had time to think, the image of my beautiful wife's smiling face popping up on the phone's glossy screen. I glanced at my work phone, set to speaker, where the guy from our New York office named Doug was explaining to the clients why we couldn't do something they had their hearts set on.

Then I lifted my cellphone to my ear and answered it.

"...don't want him calling right now, do you?" Caught mid-sentence, Emily's playful voice wasn't directed at me. And it seemed a little muffled. Confused, I slipped one white bud into my ear and tried to divide my attention between the conference call and my wife's infinitely more intriguing one.

"Unbutton your top," ordered a man's voice, even more muffled than my wife's.

That was pretty much the shortest amount of time it has ever taken for me to get it up. I sat forward, banging my knee into my desk. "You don't agree, Ian?" someone on my conference call asked. Shit, I didn't even know who that was.

I hit the mute button on my cellphone and stuttered out a response. Something like, "Sorry, I think it's a great idea," or something. My own thoughts were rolled over as I heard Emily say something about other cars. Where were they?

The more active participants in the conference call went back to whatever the hell it was they were talking about as the man's voice—Ray's, I realized—said, "My windows are tinted and no one is looking in anyway. Do it, Emily. I want to see those perfect tits."

The shock at what I was hearing was nearly equal to the shock of the scene being set for me. They were in the car...they weren't driving, right? And Emily was unbuttoning her blouse? I tried to remember what she'd been wearing when she left that morning. That tailored pink blouse, I thought, that hugged her "perfect tits."

"I knew you were a fucking wild cat, baby. You're always ready for some fun, aren't you?" It reminded me of that conversation I'd had with him so long ago, in the bar. How had the young, technical writer seen these things in my wife that I had failed to? He'd called her a *goer*. He'd recognized the wildness inside of her. And now...

"Ah, Ray... yes... your hand on my pussy feels so good." And now he was capitalizing on that awareness. I put one hand on my head as I listened, not even bothering to pay attention to the argument that had broken out on the conference call.

"You like to talk dirty, don't you?" Ray chuckled.

No, she didn't, I thought, even as she contradicted me. "Yess, ohhh…Ray…"

"Take off your panties, Emily."

"Oh, my God," I groaned, closing my eyes and seeing Emily raise her butt off the seat and drag her thong down her thighs. She'd gone out in a short, navy skirt and now that I had a little room to think, I remembered her rolling on a pair of nude thigh-highs.

"It's not that serious, Ian," my New York coworker, Doug, said on the phone—the other phone—with a chuckle.

Little did he know!

Meanwhile, Ray's voice continued to buzz in my ear. "You know what would make you even hotter?"

"What?" Emily's voice was trembling.

"You should shave everything down below." My breath caught. I stared hard at but the blinking speaker prompt on my desk phone.

"Ian, you there?"

My heart hitched for one confusing second before I realized that it was my coworker asking the question, not Ray or Emily or anyone in that car. I wanted to keep listening, but I couldn't ignore work. So as I heard my wife's breathy voice say something about her landing strip, I reassured the New York office that I was, indeed, there.

"Sorry, I'm a little distracted." My throat was parched. "What's up?"

"I think that we might be able to work something out." What the hell was he talking about?

"I'm sure," I said, forcing confidence. "He's in capable hands."

"It's not that. It's just hot, that's all." Ray's voice, weaving with Doug's in the most surreal of ways.

"That it?" I asked, my voice cracking a little. I felt sweat gather on my brow and rubbed it away with the back of my sleeve.

"I'll think... about it." Again, the overlapping conversations left me dazed. It was Emily that time, of course, her voice still thin and reedy. What was she thinking about?

The next exchange was so jumbled that I didn't comprehend any of it. Doug said something. Ray said something. And all of it against the backdrop of Emily's huffing moans. "Oh Ray... oh Ray..." Emily was close, and this one was a big one.

I needed to get off the phone. I needed to end one of these god-damn calls. "I'll call you later in the week. I need to check a few things first."

"Oh Ray!"

As my right finger hovered over the end call prompt, my left snuck under the table where I gave myself a quick rub, listening to my wife explode on the phone. I saw her in that moment, a crystal clear image: her slender body arched in the bucket seat of Ray's Mercedes, her pink blouse open, her skirt up around her waist as Ray drilled a couple fingers into her pussy.

"That's just like you, Ian. The ever-cautious one." My coworker again, interrupting the moment. Again.

Emily's voice was thin as she begged Ray to stop whatever he was doing. "No more...I can't take it..."

"That's me," I said, thankful that he couldn't see me roll my eyes. "I'll be in touch later."

I hung up before that disaster of a conversation could go any further, leaned back in my chair, and rubbed my eyes as I got my bear-ings. Here I was, sitting in my office, surrounded by my coworkers all getting work done, as my wife was fooling around with another guy. And I was hard pressed to think of another phone call that had ever gotten me this excited.

"I love making you cum," I listened to Ray say.

"I love it when you make me cum." Emily laughed, delighted. Now that the moaning had stopped and I wasn't distracted by my conference call, I realized I could hear the low grumble of a car's engine. Holy shit, they weren't just in a car. They were driving in one!

And the surprises kept coming. I heard the clank of a man's belt being undone, followed shortly by the unmistakable sound of a zipper. She wouldn't, would she?

I glanced outside. It was still light out and tinted windows only went so far. My ears strained to hear what was happening, even as my mind filled in all of the blanks. I got my confirmation a few long moments later.

"Christ, you're fucking good. Shit, Em, suck me! You're going to make me fuckin' cum, baby!"

Emily had done this for me, once upon a time, but that was late at night, and we had been parked outside her group house before I'd dropped her off. I'd always wondered what it would be like to get that treatment in a moving vehicle, but it just seemed so dangerous.

I listened harder, at last hearing the slurp as Emily's blow job got wetter. Sloppier. I heard her gag a little, punctuated by a heavy groan from what must have been a nearly delirious Ray. He was cumming. Inside of Emily's mouth.

I ran my hand across the front of my pants, just once before remembered that the fronts of our offices were constructed of glass and I had a warren of cubicles just a few feet away. My computer chimed, reminding me of yet another meeting I had—this one face-to-face in my office—and reluctantly, I ended Emily's call.

Before I had that meeting, I was going to need to rub one out in the bathroom or I wouldn't be able to think straight.

•••

That evening stretched on into eternity. All I wanted to do was grab my hot little wife and fuck her until she couldn't walk straight, but that was hardly the proper thing to do. Besides, we'd been shuffling the kids off into Natalie's care too often of late and they needed our attention. Emily didn't help matters, though, pretending that nothing happened.

"How'd your day go?" I'd ask.

"Kind of boring. Meetings, reports on those meetings, more meetings..." she'd reply with a coy smile.

"Uh, huh."

When it became clear that she was going to play coy all evening long—she wouldn't even kiss me—I decided to zone out in front of the TV and pout. I was frustrated, to say the least. I hadn't had a chance to make it to the bathroom to take care of myself before my next meeting—which started early and ended late. And after that, there were deadlines to be met and shit to be taken care of and all the while, my mind kept returning to the haunting sound of my wife's loud orgasm over the phone. Fuck!

I watched SportsCenter and left Emily alone. If she was going to be like that, so was I. I forced myself to care about this year's race for the baseball playoffs, even though my team had long since crumbled. I forced myself to tune out the sound of the shower upstairs and kept repeating that I didn't even want to join her. That was what she'd want, and I—ah, fuck, who was I kidding? I wanted to go up there just as much as she wanted me to. Somehow, I resisted.

And then Emily was there, the light of the television screen framing her like a goddess. The hard tips of her nipples cast shadows along her short, red kimono robe, which she'd only loosely belted. I licked my lips as my eyes drank in the inner swells of her breasts and her long, shapely legs.

"So what did you think of my surprise phone call today?" Her smile was bright and playful. Finally, she was acknowledging it.

I muted the TV before answering her. "It was unexpected. I didn't know what was going on…at first." I watched her shift her weight from one foot to the other. The robe opened a little more and a nipple slipped into view.

"I hope you don't mind that I took some initiative. Ray and I had a great meeting and we were feeling pretty good, and one thing led to another." I didn't need the background. I didn't need to think about their great chemistry. But still, what followed after the great meeting probably wouldn't have happened if they didn't have it.

"I loved it," I said, reaching out for her. Our fingers laced together as she slid onto the couch beside me. The short robe just barely covered her womanhood, and as she leaned back onto the couch, I caught the glistened flash of her pink lips before she crossed her legs. The robe opened more, though, and her exposed breasts quickly recaptured my attention.

"What do you think happened?" She skimmed her fingernails along the edge of her nipple.

"I know he touched you, but I want you to tell me."

"Ray…he…just started touching me." She glanced at me out of the corner of her eye and I wondered if she realized how much she lit up when she talked about him. Did she see the tumultuous emotions that caused in me?

Her caressing fingers walked down her body and slid under her robe. She bit her lip, her eyes suddenly heavy-lidded, as she touched herself.

She said, "He didn't even ask if he could."

"And you didn't try to stop him…"

"No, baby, I didn't want to." Her eyes finally shut as she began to relive the moment again. "When Ray starts touching me I get so horny. Mmmm…"

She shifted back into the couch and the silky kimono parted around her wrist. Her fingers were curled across her mound, gently running circles on the smooth folds.

"He told you to take your panties off." I watched her lips part in a silent gasp. She was thinking about Ray, and I was facilitating that. It was the hottest lesson in cause and effect I'd ever had.

"Yes, he wanted to touch my naked pussy." What had this woman done with my wife, and was she planning on staying after next week? Shamefully, I hoped that she would. "I took off my thong and stuffed it in my purse, and then he touched me again."

Emily reached out and took my hand with her free one, guiding it to her inner thigh. I took the hint, easing it between her legs. Joining her own rubbing fingers. They yielded to my touch. Was she imagining it was Ray's? Was she still lost in the fantasy?

The questions were blown away as soon as I glided up her slit and discovered that she was now clean shaven. I didn't believe my touch at first, but my eyes confirmed it. The dark strip of hair she'd always sported through our long relationship was gone. Not a single curl remained.

"You did what he wanted," I said. *He.* Ray. Now she was doing things for him; not just him doing things to her. I ran my fingertips across the bare rise. Betrayal never felt so smooth.

"Yesss…oh baby, touch me, please," she moaned.

"You're so soft." I was in stunned disbelief, but I wasn't sure what it was I was disbelieving. That my cute, innocent wife had shaved her-self bald, or that Ray had gotten her to do it? What else could he get her to do?

"Oh, baby, do you like it?" She was loving my fingers. Loving the sensitivity.

God yes, I did. I'd wanted her to sport this look forever, but was too afraid to ask for it. She got touchy at times. "It feels so different... yes...honey...yes..."

Emily reached over with her left hand and started rubbing me through my shorts. I glanced at her. At what we were doing. Was this the scene in the Ray's car? Was this what a passing car might have witnessed if they could have seen through Ray's tinted windows? I swelled at the thought. My wife seemed to want to be touched a cer-tain way and didn't let go of my hand on her until I got it right. When I tapped across her clit, she went crazy.

"He...rubbed my pussy...just like that...Ian..."

She looked so exposed like that. Her hooded button sat swol-len and proud in a sea of glistening flesh. I made a circuit around it, touching the edges. Pushing her closer. Faster.

"He made you cum, didn't he?" I said it for Emily—to spur the fantasy playing out behind her eyelids.

No, not fantasy. *Memory.*

"Yes...yes...YES!"

I curled two fingers across her swollen lips, keeping my thumb and the heel of my hand pressed up against her mons. I turned into her, collecting her head with my free hand and pulling her in for a fierce kiss. As my tongue passed between her lips, I corkscrewed two fingers into her pussy. She was so wet as she writhed on my hand. So wet.

At last, she pushed me away and shed her robe. The dirty talk continued.

"Do you know what I did after he made me cum?" Pushing up onto her knees, she pulled my head into her soft cleavage. I sought out a nipple, swirling it in my mouth. Emily moaned.

"You blew him."

She released my cock and looked up at me from my lap, one dark brow arched. God, this was all so familiar, yet incredibly foreign at the same time. Dark, blow-dried hair cascading around her pale, freckled face.

"Did you mind me sucking his cock?" She knew exactly what she was doing; exactly how fucking dirty that sounded. It made my blood boil.

"No..." I groaned as she spit a dollop of saliva on my cock and stroked it in. That was new. So much of this was new! "Fuck you're hot, Emily... oh God..."

She wasted no more time. Satisfied that I was wet enough, she swallowed me. Heat licked up my neck and across my scalp. Did Ray do this, I thought as I ground my teeth and began pumping my hips back into her. When she tried to regain control, I grabbed her thick hair and forced her back down. Forced her to stroke harder and deeper. I felt my cock push against the back of her mouth and heard her choke. Had she choked on Ray?

"Ahhh...suck it...suck it you hot cocksucker..."

I grunted as I jammed my cock head into her throat. Did she do this for fucking Ray?! When she tried to pull away, I held her in place, not even bothering to guide her head up and down. My driving hips were all the movement needed. My balls tightened and suddenly, everything got light. Weightless. Emily got her head free, but not before I erupted all over her face. The first rope of creamy white got her on the cheek. Then across her nose. Just below her eye. Her chin. She opened her mouth to catch the remaining jism, but the mess had already been made.

Spent at last, all that pent up fervor dissipated. Suddenly, I realized what I'd done. Jesus, what had I done?! I looked down at Emily's face, dripping with my cum, as she looked back up at me like I was a stranger.

"Are you okay?" she asked, although she might as well have said, *What the fuck is wrong with you?!* "Are *we* okay?"

"Yeah…yeah," I said, looking away. What had come over me?

Emily was always the persistent one. "Ian, look at me." Her voice was soft. Even tempered. Maybe a little scared. "Are we okay?"

What? How could she ask that? After all that we've gone through, how could she? I forced myself to look back at her. Back at her face, covered in my cum. She didn't seem angry…

"Yeah, we're okay. I guess I just got carried away," I added sheepishly.

"If this game with Ray is too much, I want you to tell me. We can stop this all right now."

"No!" That wasn't it at all. Oddly enough, Ray was just the catalyst for something that had wanted to get out for who knows how long. If anything, I wanted it to continue. "No, I don't want to stop. I'm sorry if I got too rough."

Emily surprised me with a smile. Now it was her turn to look away, shy. "I kind of liked it, actually."

"Really?"

More discoveries. More new turns.

"Really, it was. I have to admit, I like the way you've been looking at me since we started *playing*." She looked back at me, her face pink. "God, I must look like a mess right now." She wiped some of the cum from her cheek and rubbed it between her fingers. Then, with an evil glint in her eyes, she sucked her finger between her lips.

"A hot mess.

" I laughed.

"Oh? You like seeing your cum on my face?" She glanced down, where I was fisting an erection that was already beginning to rise again.

"It's like I'm watching you transform before my eyes," I whispered as she wiped the rest of my cum from her face with my t-shirt.

"Into what?" She asked, equally curious and nervous. Her hand covered mine and we stroked the saliva and cum mixture along the hardening length. I wasn't sure how to answer that question. A radiant, sexual creature? A...slut?

"I…" She didn't let me answer.

It was as though her need had finally consumed her. Impatiently, she crawled into my lap and kissed me. I could hear the high-pitched ring of the muted television. I could hear the quiet of the room come alive and join the heat of the moment. My hands slipped into the hollow of her back and grasped her round ass. With a single down stroke, I buried myself ball-deep in her pussy with a groan.

She steadied herself with a hand on either shoulder, leaned back, and undulated into my lap. This wasn't lovemaking. It wasn't even dirty teasing. The foreplay was over; the sex talk was finished. This was raw, unadulterated fucking.

I watched a trickle of sweat roll off her collarbone and through the valley of her breasts. I watched it cross her flat stomach, circumnavigate her navel, and run its course across her newly clean-shaven mound. My heart jumped at that still unfamiliar look. Our union seemed even more lewd: all that pale skin stretching around my girth, her clitoris swollen and exposed. I watched myself slide in and out of her until she dug her nails into my shoulders. I looked up just in time to see her orgasm. She threw her head back, closed her eyes, and shuddered around my cock.

More rivulets of sweat joined the first. Perspiration beaded her body. It beaded mine. I lifted her familiar-yet-new body up and down, my guiding hands groping her backside, and watched her ride out her orgasm. She opened her eyes. It was like being struck by a thunderbolt. She saw me, and I saw her. I saw conflict and confusion there, but also love. Devotion. Affection. She was Emily. My Emily. And she watched me with open eyes as I found my own release.

I shuddered as I filled her. She didn't join me, but seemed to enjoy the feeling regardless. She bit her lip, pulled me tight against her bosom, and ground on my pulsating member.

Emily kissed me happily once I was through. Her sweeping bangs were plastered against her forehead and her freckled skin glistened. I kissed her neck, tasting the salt of her, and she climbed off.

"Looks like I'm going to need another shower." She giggled, sounding tired.

I agreed.

CHAPTER 11

Nervousness followed me throughout the day—nervousness like a kid climbing the rungs of the highest diving board at the local pool, each plastic and aluminum step creaking under his fingers.

I'd been thinking a lot about pools lately. They haunted my dreams, filling them with wet, chlorinated hallucinations—not all of which were unpleasant. I'd close my eyes and see silhouettes in the dancing lights that escaped the surface of the water.

But today, the analogy served a different purpose. As I ascended the high dive, I felt the rush of adrenaline along with the buzz of danger. I'd never been up there and I wasn't entirely sure what I'd do when I was.

Emily was up to something. I could see it in the way she stared at me that morning. It was almost palpable in her silence. When I saw her e-mail in my personal inbox, my suspicions were confirmed, although I still wasn't sure what was going on. All I knew was that it would be more intense than yesterday. Crazier than the phone call. Things were escalating and it was Emily doing the escalating.

At the beginning of this whole game, it had been my own actions that drove things. I'd quizzed Ray about Emily. I'd set the two of them up so I could watch them flirt. I'd even been the one who convinced Emily that it was okay to flirt a little more. But now, it was Emily behind the wheel. She'd been behind it during our second night at Bar 88. She'd set up the phone call yesterday. And now...she was up to something.

I didn't know how I felt about that—about losing control of something I barely had control of in the first place. It scared the shit out of me, yet I didn't want to stop. We'd come this far. I wanted to see it through to the end, and as reluctant as Emily sometimes seemed to be, I think she wanted this, too.

I left work early, told Natalie that I needed to take a work conference call upstairs, and slipped into our bedroom.

I felt buoyed by my blood pressure, driven forward by that *thump thump* crashing between my ears. I didn't need to pull up Emily's instructions to know what to do—I'd read that e-mail again and again throughout the day—but it still felt surreal.

I set the computer on the desk in our bedroom and logged into Emily's office conferencing system. My fingers shook as I typed in the password she'd given me. My gut churned when Emily popped onto the computer screen.

She must have touched up her make-up since she'd left home. Her lips seemed glossier. Her hair was brushed out. She was beautiful.

"I'm doing this for you, honey, so I hope you enjoy the show."

She reached for the tie of her sea-green wrap blouse and eased it off her shoulder.

My eyes went wide. I glanced at the bedroom door, which was only half closed. I could hear the kids downstairs, playing with Natalie—thought about closing it, too, but didn't want to miss a thing.

I recognized the frilly green bra that caressed and lifted her freckled swells. She'd worn it on one of our first Christmases, before the gifts were extravagant. She'd given herself that year and the green lingerie was the wrapper, complete with a little satin bow dangling between her breasts. She was enjoying the tease as much as I was.

"What are you up to? Where are you?"

"I'm in one of the video conference suites at the office. Just about everyone's left for the day and no one knows I'm here." She neatly folded her blouse and set it on one of the high-backed leather chairs that surrounded the round, polished wooden tables.

The charcoal slacks went next, unveiling the matching green panties, bikini-cut with satin ribbons on her hips. Good girl, I thought as she made sure to slide back into her three-inch heels once her pants were off. She was a present, alright, just not for me this time...

I thought about her statement earlier: *I'm doing this for you...*

She obviously believed it, but did I?

"No one knows you're there?" I asked, feeling my heart heave in my chest.

"Well, *someone* knows I'm here." Her face glowed. "I told him to meet me in here and he should be around any minute now. I'd better turn off the monitor." She glanced at the camera one last time before picking up the remote.

"Wait."

Emily had always been the one with a stronger moral compass; it constantly felt like I was the one doing pressuring. The quickness of the current situation felt weird and I wasn't sure how I felt about it. One thing was certain, though. She was having fun.

"I love you," I said.

Emily's face softened. "I love you too, honey."

We might as well have been in the same room, sharing that lovers' gaze. I felt warmth well up inside of me. Those looks had come too far and few between.

"I'll see you when I get home." With that, she switched me off.

Her forethought was what had me most surprised. Emily was definitely no longer a passive participant in this game. She'd set up the room. She'd sent me instructions on what to do and arranged for Natalie to stay longer. She'd even brought in a roll of black electrical tape to cover up the indicator light.

All for me? Yeah right.

I couldn't get a handle on all the facts. Not yet. Even as I watched Emily on the high definition feed wearing next-to-nothing in her office, it didn't seem real. It was too outlandish. On an intellectual level, I knew what she was about to do. Emotionally... well, emotionally, I felt queasy sense that we were about to pass the point of no return. My stomach kept flipping. Pressure kept building.

Emily and I both jumped when someone knocked on the door. Three hard raps. She glanced at the camera hesitantly, as though seeking some kind of nod of approval, then turned to the door. I wanted to reach out and touch her shoulder. I wanted to reassure her.

In heels, her taut buttocks looked nearly perfect, a plush, inverted heart that was barely covered by the dark green lace of the bikini panties. I remembered pulling open those bows at her hips. How long would it take for Ray to do the same? The heat of that question sizzled along my scalp. *Careful, careful, Ian...*I stood up and paced the room, running my hands through my hair again and again.

I thought back to Bobby's wedding last year, when I'd first experienced the bittersweet taste of these moments. I was like a junkie, trying to relive the rush of my first hit. My teeth clattered. My body shook. I was both hot and cold and numb and so fucking ready for this. I closed the door, shutting the domestic sounds of my children. They had no place in this dark story.

"I hoped it would be a nice surprise."

I was drawn back to the computer with my heart in my throat

and sweat on my brow. Emily was standing away from Ray, her smile bringing out her high cheekbones and the green-brown in her eyes. I was seeing Emily look at Ray in the same way she'd looked at me, way back when we'd first started seeing one another. The freshness was back. The sense of adventure.

It scared the shit out of me.

"You can say that again. Damn, Emily, you're full of fucking surprises."

I'd done this. My scalp continued to prickle. I'd practically shoved these two into a closet and locked the door.

"I guess you just bring it out in me." I sucked in air but it wasn't enough to fill my collapsing lungs. "Come here and kiss me hello."

I'd probably watched the two of them kiss half a dozen times already, but I still burned me up inside. The mics were powerful enough to capture it all, from the wet smacks of their lips to creak of the conference table beneath her. I swore I could almost hear the sound of his fingers sliding across her panty-clad ass. Emily accepted him as their bodies melted together, falling in his arms, and squealed happily when he lifted her up. She wrapped her legs around him and tipped her head back to give him access to her neck. He manhandled her with such ease. Did she like that? I thought about last night and how I'd controlled her. It was a side of Emily that had never come out until now.

And there was the other thing. The insecurity part of all of this. I couldn't have held her up so effortlessly, for so long. I was in good shape, but I'd never been built like Ray.

He looked into her cleavage. "I thought you were having second thoughts after you blew me off earlier."

Emily chanced a look in my direction before replying. That was nice. I chuckled at my feelings of inadequacy, preening like she'd just given me a generous compliment. Maybe all of this *was* for me…

"I was just saving it all for now," she said, looking back at him. They kissed loosely. "You can't have everything you want whenever you want it, baby. You can't always be in control." Was she talking to me as much as she was talking to Ray?

"I don't mind when a woman takes charge."

Emily giggled as he inhaled her, nibbling along the soft skin of her neck. I could hear their soft kisses and her hushed sighs. It was like being in the room with them. It was so crystal clear. It was the sexiest torture I'd ever felt.

"Careful," she breathed. "Don't leave any marks for me to explain to my husband."

I laughed to myself, leaning on my arm and stretching out my legs. She knew her audience well.

"I'll try to return you in one piece." The tenderness Ray showed as he set her back on the table unnerved me all over again. My laughter still hung in the air, but I no longer felt like laughing. Hot to cold. Quick as flicking a switch.

She pulled off his shirt and devoured his upper body. That was hard to watch. I almost looked away, not wanting to see the way she ran her hands across the smooth bulges of his pecs and down his rippling six pack. Not wanting to believe her heavy-lidded desire.

Bowing forward, she kissed his chest and flicked her tongue across his nipple. Her fingers lingered on his abs as Ray's returned to her hair. When she sucked his nipple into her mouth, they tightened. The power shifted. He pulled her face back to his. Emily curled her tongue out to tease him, licking his lips before his deep kiss enveloped her.

My cock was hard. My face was hot. My breathing was short. Things were slipping away from me. Or had they already, long ago?

Ray grabbed her breasts, mashing them together. Emily moaned as he pinched and rolled her nipples through the soft lace.

"Mmmm, Ray..." Reaching behind her, she unhooked her bra. Ray yanked it off and threw it at the camera before quickly returning to her nipples, now exposed. She arched her back as he tweaked her, lost in the sensations.

Incredibly, Emily pushed him away.

"Wait… wait…" she whimpered. She'd already built up a sheen of sweat and was breathing heavily through her nostrils. The heaves in her chest only made her naked breasts look even more tantalizing. She latched onto his thick shoulders as she slid off the table and shifted him around, looking up at him through her thick lashes. As she began to unbuckle his belt, understanding dawned on him, and another set of nerves flowed through me.

Emily pulled Ray's cock out, thick and fully erect. I slid my hand into my shorts and stroked my own erection. When I'd watched them by the pool, it had been dark and I had been too far to catch the details. When I'd listened to them in the car, it was only sounds, made more confusing by my parallel conversation.

But now those barriers were gone. There was no use denying that my sweet Emily was really into this. She swept her hair over one shoulder, tucking it back over her ear, and I could clearly see it on her face. On the way her eyes never left Ray's.

I both hated and loved the way she looked at me as she wrapped her hand around the base of his cock. At first, when this whole game had started, I got off on the egocentric idea of another man wanting my wife. But now, I had to admit that there was more to it than that. I'd gotten my validation that Emily was hot a long time ago. Guys like Ray really did want her. So why was this all still so arousing?

As she swirled the head of Ray's cock, I began to develop an answer. It was hazy and half-formed and the visual stimuli was making it hard to concentrate on it. Ray saw her as sexy—he'd always seen her as sexy. It was *me* who was seeing it again, as though for the first time.

When the head of Ray's cock was nice and shiny, she took the tip in, rocking it against the roof of her mouth.

"Oh, Emm..." He leaned back on his elbows. Emily eased more of him into her mouth, watching him as she relaxed her jaw and stretching her mouth around his thickness. She was slow about it, swallowing him until he touched the back of her throat, then pulling off him with a loud pop. She giggled delightfully before repeating it.

"You do that so well," he grunted as she licked along the outside again. "You are the hottest fucking thing I've ever seen. Ohhh, fuck, baby..."

Pushing his shaft against his stomach, she lowered her mouth to his balls, bathing them in her spit before swallowing them, one at a time. It was so deviant of her. So disconnected from the mother of my kids who balked whenever I'd ask her to wear something short and tight.

"Fuck... shit... you're sucking my balls! You're sucking my fucking balls, Em..."

She swirled them with her tongue one last time before tonguing back up the sensitive underbelly of his cock.

"Spit on it," he grunted, sweeping her hair out of her face. "Do it, dirty girl."

Emily giggled, smiling up at him as she spit on the purple head obediently. I thought of last night when I'd called her a *cocksucker*. The more I dug, hotter she got. By the time he was done with her, how many lines will she have crossed? I hated that deep down, I hoped it would be many.

She rubbed her saliva in with both her hands, leaning forward and lapping across the tip again. Her eyes were locked with Ray's and her smile was so fucking wicked. When she ducked back down, she sucked him hard and fast. The slow tease was gone.

He moaned, pushing his hips off the table to meet her bobbing mouth. His face went slack, his eyelids fluttering. He was close and Emily wasn't slowing down. The slurping sound filled the conference room, mixed with Ray's moans. He grabbed Emily's head and pulled her back at the last second. I thought he was going to blow his load all over her face. Emily did, too, practically squealing as she looked up at him.

"You're not getting off that easy tonight, Em," Ray huffed, hopping down from the table. He lifted Emily up and put her in his spot. I stiffened. Was he going to…?

"But…" Emily protested, suddenly as tense as I was. Almost as though she'd read my mind, she glanced quickly at the camera. Our eyes met, although she couldn't have known it. My apprehension was reflected in her eyes. Were we ready for this?

I was drowning again, choking as I watched them from the bottom of the pool. It was colder down here. I heard Emily's moans, muffled in my ears as I fought to focus. Ray didn't immediately fuck her. He kissed her hard and went to work on her tits again. He sucked each nipple, drawing them out. She moaned his name and I had the hazy sense to turn the volume of the laptop down a couple notches.

My cock was in my hand. I don't know when I got it out or how long I'd been stroking it, but it was there, rigid and shameful. I felt jittery. My teeth chattered as I watched them. As I watched Ray's hands finally pull the bows of her panties loose. Was this it? His cock must have been resting there between her thighs. When I had unwrapped her, so many years ago, I hadn't wasted any time. Was he going to?

"Ray… no… we can't…"

Disappointment? Was that disappointment that had registered in me? How could I be both relieved and upset?

Ray didn't pause a beat, although he looked annoyed. Did Emily catch that? I didn't think so. She was too busy lolling her head back as he kissed down her flat belly, pulling the panties away. His hands returned to her breasts, tweaking her high-seated nipples. She spread her legs open until her knees were resting on the polished conference table. I could watch Ray's mouth walk down her tummy and his eyes alight on her bare pussy.

"Did you do this for me?" he asked with a smile.

"I...I..."

He kissed her clean shaven mound, softly probing between her lips with his tongue. "Did you?"

"Yes..." I knew that was the answer, yet still it still made me anxious to hear her say it. She'd shaved herself for the first time in her life for Ray. Not for me. That made him real again. He had desires of his own. He was the X-factor in our little game. What else was he capable of getting her to do?

Her young lover spread her lips open with his hands and dragged his tongue along her swollen furrow. Arching her back and groaning loudly, she splayed out across the conference table and I drank it all in as I stroked myself. She was all curves and shivering flesh as Ray worked her. He teased her, driving her the edge and yanking her back.

Could she really believe that she was doing this for me? Could I? My faith was being tested as she screamed his name and begged for more. But maybe she was. In the past, she'd worn sexy outfits for me. She'd even gone topless one afternoon on a beach in Southern France. Was this all that different?

"OH GOD OH GOD!" she screamed, hammering the table as her orgasm pummeled her. He had two fingers drilling her and she was thrusting back. "RAY! OH RAY!"

This was different. Ray made it different. It was a dangerous thought. And yet I was on the edge of my own orgasm. I backed off, even as she came. The sight nearly drove me over the edge. All it took was a glance over at Ray and the way he was surveying her writhing body and I was stopped cold. As much as I wanted to believe he was nothing more than a plaything, he wasn't. He was another man, not only with feelings, but someone that a girl could have feeling *for*. Did my wife?

He fisted his cock and climbed up onto the conference table. All pretense fell away. All my lust-fueled justifications. The air felt thick. Oppressive. I couldn't breathe. Ray placed his dick against Emily's slick lips. This was it. My cock lurched in my encircling fingers. Bile rose up in my stomach. And then—

"Ray! No!" Emily's eyes were open. She was trying to close her legs. A desire to protect her overwhelmed me. If she didn't want this, then I didn't either. I sat up, riveted, half-thinking about storming in to her rescue. I glanced at my dresser, where my keys sat in their tray.

"Cut the shit, Em. I know you want it. It's all over your face. I know you want to fuck me."

Incredibly, he was right. Her eyes fluttered as he sawed his thickness along her wet furrow. I felt...betrayed. I sank back onto the bed, all heroic emotions banished.

"Ray, no. I can't...my husband..."

I can't always be your excuse, Emily. I felt bitter. Bitter at being used.

"If you were so worried about your husband, you wouldn't be here with me."

He was right. Those strange feelings from last night returned. She needed to be taught a lesson. Or maybe the lesson was for me?

"I just can't, Ray. Please! Anything else…please…"

"I'm not going to force you, but I don't believe you don't want it," Ray huffed. He was a better man than I was feeling right now. He loosened his grip on her thigh and sat up on his knees.

Emily's panic shifted as she realized he was telling the truth. "Ray, I'm sorry." She was afraid she'd lose him. *Someone a girl could have feeling for…* That look, more than the idea of Ray burying his cock inside of her, hurt me.

"I'm not some toy for you to tease, Em. We're not going to keep doing this if you're not serious. I want that sweet little pussy of yours and you won't be here if you didn't want to give it to me. Just let go."

Emily reached down, grabbing his cock. Their eyes met. Emily bit her lip. She didn't even need to say anything. She just needed to pull him forward a little, to spread her legs back apart and place him against her.

"I'm sorry, I'm not trying to tease you." Her voice was genuine. Emotional. This had gone far beyond the game we'd started. She forced a smile. "There are other ways I can make you feel good."

She was really upset that she'd let Ray down. She felt something for him. The twinge I felt in my stomach was jealousy. Pure and hard and scary. How much danger is too much danger? Incredibly, my cock, still hard, seemed to think we still weren't there.

"You give a great blow job, but I want more. I want it all."

"I don't know what to say." The moment was so pure—so intimate. I looked away, feeling wrong for witnessing it. This wasn't Emily my wife and her boy-toy. These two were sharing something profound.

Ray pulled her off the table and pushed her to her knees. The intimacy was still there, brutal and beautiful. Ray yanked her head back by the hair, punishing her. He fed her his cock and she took it, wrapping those beautiful lips around the veiny girth. She didn't blow him. No, Ray was in total control, pulling her back and forth and using her.

I was there with them again. I was in Ray's spot, yanking her head across my erection. This was her lesson to learn and Ray's to give, but I wished it was me. He thrust harder and deeper into her mouth. She gagged as he must have entered her throat. He didn't stop. If anything, he fucked her even wilder. Emily's nostrils flared as she moaned out again, getting off on the abuse. The vibrations must have set Ray off, too. Suddenly, cum was running down her chin, dripping onto her breasts.

I exploded with them, barely getting my hand up to shield me from a sticky mess. I looked away, nearly closed the laptop. Even as my balls emptied, my cock remained hard. Hard and agitated. As I stood and went into the bathroom to grab some tissues, my eyes slid along the pictures that lined our wall. Pictures of a perfect family unit. We still had that, right?

Ray was talking when I emerged: "I don't know if you're playing some kind of game with me, but game time is over, Em."

I didn't go back to the monitor. For some reason, it felt wrong to watch it any more. The fun and games were over.

He continued. "I like you a lot, but we're both adults here and we know how these things go. You can't play the virginal waif with me. Don't keep going down this road if you're not ready for where it leads. I want you, and I'll be here when you're ready."

"Ray... Ray..." Emily sounded stricken. I wished I was there to hold her. To soothe her and let her know that it would be alright. I heard a door shut. I listened a moment longer, and when I checked again, the conference feed blinked, DISCONNECTED.

CHAPTER 12

A couple years ago, I was on the roof, patching up some rotting shingles when I slipped and fell to the concrete sidewalk along the side of the house. I was lucky and walked away with nothing more than a bruised hip and the memory of the fall. It probably took less than a second for me to reach the ground, yet I could remember more details of that moment than I usually held onto in an entire week.

I remember the panic in my gut as I began to skid, thinking, *This isn't going to be good.*

I remember turning back and trying to grab the gutter—too late.

I remember the full rotation I made. How I looked out across our yard, at the way our neighbor's sprinkler soaked the side of our silver minivan. How Jenny's pink and purple bicycle sat in the middle of the front yard and how I needed to talk to her about putting it away.

Every detail, immortalized in super slow motion.

The hour of Emily's commute after she shut down the video feed felt exactly the same as falling off that roof. Everything slowed down. Every detail was immortalized. The way Emily and Ray kissed and how comfortable that had become for them. I could close my eyes and visualize each downy hair in the small of her back, and how Ray trailed his fingers across the dimples above her ass when he pulled her close. Each image twisted my gut and pushed a little more air out of my lungs, but they wouldn't stop. And I didn't want them to.

Our nanny had fixed the kids an early supper. I'd sent her home and put them to bed myself, kissing each softly on the forehead before shutting the door. But behind my eyes, the details of the night played on. Emily's coy look through her long lashes. Emily sinking to her knees. Emily's squeal each time the wet flesh of his cock popped from her mouth.

I fixed her a dinner and barely touched my own. I didn't trust myself to hold anything down and was wary of the nauseous buzz that radiated from my gut. I kept whispering, "Okay then..." Over and over. Yet I had no idea what was *okay*, and what words should come next.

Was it time to stop? As I covered Emily's dinner in foil, I thought of my wife on her back, her naked body glistened with sweat, her legs open for Ray. In her hand, she held him, swollen and thick and so close to a line she hadn't crossed yet. Christ, I was burning. I felt sweat trickle down my spine under my t-shirt and when I rubbed my brow with my hand, it came away damp.

"Okay then..."

I tried to imagine the conversation that put the brakes on this game. I realized I didn't want to have it. As potentially destructive as it was, I wanted to risk it. I didn't want to stop.

Emily found me in the kitchen, her heels clicking on the hardwood floors. She held her purse limply at her side and looked tired, studying me cockeyed.

"Kids asleep?" she asked.

I nodded, telling her I'd fixed her dinner, although I didn't remember the details of what I'd said even a moment later. I was too busy looking at her, thinking how beautiful she was. Seeing her as

Ray saw her. The silky green blouse was back in place, wrapped tightly across her bosom.

Tension took on the form of a high decibel buzz that I couldn't shake. I wondered if this was what it felt like just before someone was struck by lightning.

Emily pulled the foil of her dinner away, looking down at the soggy potatoes and grilled chicken breast, and almost started crying.

"It's over, Ian. I can't do this again."

I rose out of my chair and was behind in her a second. I touched her shoulders and she flinched. "Emily, honey, try to calm down."

"Ian, I'm sorry about tonight. I didn't plan on that happening. Oh God…" She sniffed hard, her eyes glued to her dinner plate like it held a message she could decipher if only she stared long enough. She didn't turn to look back at me.

She didn't plan on that happening? That was bullshit. She'd known exactly what she was doing. She'd greeted Ray in her fucking bra and panties. I was glad she couldn't see the look on my face. It made it easier to remain calm. To pretend like I understood her at all. "Don't be sorry. You were amazing tonight."

This time, she *did* turn and look up at me, her brow tight with confusion. My smile wasn't completely forced. I mean, she *had* been amazing. The thought of her performance had me stirring once again. But all this denial she had going on was starting to grate.

"But…at the end…I almost…didn't you see…"

I stepped around her and leaned against the edge of our dining room table. "Emily, everything was great."

She didn't take my hands at first.

I continued. "I don't understand what you're so upset about." I didn't add, *how else did you expect it to end?* "You were incredible tonight."

"Why aren't you upset?" How could *she* be agitated at *me*?

"Me? Why would I be upset? You blew me away tonight, Em. I knew you were up to something, but—"

"I almost fucked another man! Is that okay with you? Is that what you really want?"

Her flaring rage caught me by surprise. After all, it wasn't me who'd invited Ray into a private conference room after hours?

"Emily…" I reached down for her hand, but she pulled it away.

"Is it? Was that the plan? Do you want to watch me fuck someone else?"

"What the fuck, Emily? You set up this whole thing up today, not me!"

She bolted out of her seat and started to stomp away, but I grabbed her. Squeezed her arm until she flinched. We rarely fought like this, but the adrenaline felt good—felt different than the helpless anxiety that was overwhelming me. I felt violent. Brash. I held it in check as best as I could, but it escaped through my clenched teeth. "Don't pretend this has all been about me. I see how you are with him. I know that you want Ray."

She turned her head just enough to regard me out of the corner of her eye. I'd found the exposed nerve and struck it hard.

"Don't you see how dangerous this is? How wrong it is?" she asked.

The anger that had been boiling beneath the surface calmed down to a simmer. This, I could work with. I released my grip on her arm and stepped up behind her, pulling her soft hair back from her neck.

I said, "I don't see anything wrong. All I see is how sexy you are and how this experience has made our marriage hotter than it's been in years. Why do you want to stop now?"

"Because I'm afraid things will go too far!" she whisper-shouted between her gritting teeth.

If she really believed that, she wasn't just lying to me and Ray, but to herself as well. I wanted to shake reason into her. "I don't think you're afraid things will go too far. I think you're afraid because you *want* them to go too far."

"What?" she asked, once again trying to pull free. I grabbed her by the hips, holding her tight against me. She didn't struggle, but she watched me warily over her shoulder. I could see her turning my words over in her head. She felt so slim and fragile in my arms. My adrenaline surged once again. I traced my hands up her stomach and scooped up her breasts. I could feel her nipples against the palms of my hands. Whatever tumultuous feelings she was having, lust was one of them.

"You're not mad at me." My thick breath washing across the small hairs just behind her ear. My right hand rose further, digging across the sweaty plane of her upper chest before wrapping around her neck. I didn't squeeze, I didn't choke, but part of me wanted to. I was caught off guard by a sadistic side that I didn't recognize. A side that felt the pulse of her blood under her paper-thin skin and the short, gasping breaths she took, and wanted to sink my teeth in. "You're mad at yourself because you want this as much as I do."

I didn't let her respond. I didn't trust myself if she tried to deny it any longer. I turned her face to mine and kissed her hard, forcing my tongue down her throat. At first, she struggled. That only turned me on more. I held her tight against me, rocking my hips against her as I powered down against her lips. The fight in her weakened and when I was sure she wouldn't flee if I let go, I released her. Before she could turn to face me, though, I tore open her blouse. She exhaled in husky surprise.

We undressed each other hastily, right there in the kitchen. We'd never done it in this kitchen before—our sexual life had normalized by the time we moved into this bigger home and it had just never come up. I don't think Emily realized where she even was until I had her bent over the kitchen table and I'd slid my cock into her incredibly damp pussy. By that time, she didn't care. She just cried out and let herself be taken.

"You're so fucking hot, Em." I steadied myself, driving my hips against her firm buttocks. "I don't want to stop. I don't want to go back to before."

"God…Ian…don't stop…"

Our heavy wooden tables shifted, scrapping loudly across the floor. I watched as my clutching hands made white imprints on her flesh and felt the urge—for the first time in my life—to spank her. Only fear of waking the kids stayed my hand.

Was Emily imagining me behind her? Or Ray?

"You want to fuck him, don't you?" The question emerged gruff. I knew the answer.

"Ian…" she pleaded as I imagined what she must have been seeing. What she must have been imagining. Ray behind her, naked and hard, filling her pussy with his strange, unfamiliar cock.

"Say it! Tell me you want to fuck him!"

"Ian…I…I…" I needed to hear it. I needed to fucking hear my cock-sucking wife say the words. To finally own up to the truth—"Yes!" she howled. "I want to fuck Ray! Ohhh…is that what you want to hear?"

She tried to rise up, to look back at me, but I held her down, pinned to the table and squirming on my cock. I grunted for more. Wanted to hear her say more. She gave it to me. Gave it to me in spades.

"I want him! I wanted to fuck him today…I wanted him inside me… God…I want his cock!"

Each word fell like a bolt of lightning that left me sizzling and dazed and so fucking high. I pounded her faster and harder. The kitchen table creaked and groaned under us. I wondered if it would break. Fuck, I wanted to break it.

"Tell me… say it…"

Sweat dripped off my forehead onto her sweeping back, mixing with her own heavy perspiration.

"Fuck me… fuck me…" Each time she begged, I rammed her. "Fuck me, Ray! FUCK ME RAY!"

I felt her pussy collapse around me as I exploded inside of her, flooding her with my heat. She had her cheek to the table, eyes closed, and I knew without a doubt that she was thinking of Ray inside her, not me. The rush that I'd been searching for since I'd first watched Emily dance with that young groomsman was there, ten times as strong. I knew then that I couldn't stop until it wasn't just a fantasy.

I helped her up. We gathered our things and headed for the bedroom before the kids came out to investigate. "You really do want to fuck him, don't you?"

"I don't know what to say, Ian."

After all that, why did I suddenly feel nervous? Why was my heart fluttering? We didn't bother putting our clothes back on, instead deciding to make a quick dash for the bedroom. I made sure to follow her from behind as we went up the stairs, drinking in her long, naked body.

"Say you'll do it."

"What?" She glanced back over her shoulder. I prodded her on before answering.

"I know you want to fuck Ray and I want to see you do it, so finally just admit the truth." There. The thing she'd been trying to get me to say since the beginning, out in the open. I felt exposed. Vulnerable.

"You really want me to sleep with another man?" At last, in the bedroom, we shut the door behind us.

I felt safe again. "I doubt there will be much sleeping."

She rolled her eyes and patted my chest. "This is no time to be funny." She went onto her toes and kissed me softly. "You're saying you really want to see me having sex with Ray?"

I wrapped my arms around her and held her close. She rested her head on my shoulder. "I think this is something we all want."

"But I don't think I can. It's going too far…"

"Is it really? I think you're just rationalizing." I was pushing. I knew I should probably stop while I was ahead, but I couldn't. "You've sucked his cock. He's gone down on you. We all want this, so it's silly to pretend we don't."

"Maybe I'm rationalizing, but it doesn't feel right."

I took her hand and led her to the bed. "None of this felt right in the beginning, did it?"

"No."

We climbed in under the covers. "But then you gave yourself to the experience and you've loved every second. So why deny yourself the ultimate indulgence?"

She was silent a long time, but I took some comfort in the fact that she was snuggling against me rather than turning away. "So you really want this?" She sounded tired.

"Yes. So do you." Why did it seem so hard to make her see the truth? Why was she living in denial?

I was relieved when she finally let that go. "Yes, I want to have sex with Ray, but I could live without doing it. I'll do it, but I want you to understand—I am doing this for you." She leveled her eyes at me.

"I'm going to fuck Ray, and I know I'll enjoy it, but I am going to do it for you."

If that was the white lie she chose to tell herself, I could live with that, too.

"Okay."

She shifted one last time before reaching behind her and shutting off the light. Exhausted, we fell asleep in one another's arms.

CHAPTER 13

After the decision had been made, things entered hyper speed. Emily talked to Ray the next day, casually bringing it up as I prepared dinner. He'd invited her over that Saturday to help him pack. Or that was the pretext. I thought it was kind of funny that they still needed an excuse.

"So are you going over there?" I asked.

"I said I would, unless you don't want me to."

I bristled at that. It felt less like she was checking on my state-of-mind and more like she was trying to pass responsibility. I focused on the carrots I was cutting. "No, you should go. I really want you to."

"Don't worry. I'll be bringing you along...sort of."

I learned what *sort of* meant later that night. Last week, before we'd ever talked about how far the game would go, she'd purchased a purse-camera. That struck a chord in my gut, tense yet exciting. The Burberry purse looked like any other, but housed a pin-hole camera, microphone, and transmitter. The device came with a receiver that looked like a GPS device and could pick up the signal from the purse. She said the battery life was around two hours.

I was pretty shocked that she'd taken this initiative. I didn't need any more evidence that she was a willing participant in this game of ours, but here was the smoking gun. Her eagerness was frightening and awe-inspiring all at once. We had wild, loud sex that night, where she shared with me in excruciatingly graphic detail how she'd given Ray a blow job in the front seat of his car after they'd talked. A couple months ago, we'd never shared more than a few dirty words between us—a hushed *cock* in the dark, or a demure *fuck me* when she was close. Now she was moaning how she'd taken another man's cock out and sucked it as I fucked her hard.

We were playing with fire, for sure, but that definitely had benefits.

•••

The days leading up to Saturday were hot and feverish. The bridge of this song had passed; now it was all crescendo, each day rising until the only thing I could focus on were thoughts of Ray and Emily. It was all I talked about. I didn't know what I did at work other than that I got up in the morning and went there and came home in the evening.

Emily was similarly insatiable. We were all over each other, paying Natalie overtime just to keep the kids busy long enough for us to fuck when we were home. Dinner passed in a blur and we were fucking again. As I drilled her into the mattress and she cried beneath me, eyes closed, I knew she was thinking of him. Of what he'd do to her. And that made me take her even harder.

By Friday, things were at their peak. I felt the wild energy crackle like heat lightning in the synapses of my brain. I couldn't think straight and I sure as hell couldn't focus. I took the afternoon off and nursed a beer at a bar on the way home. I blinked my eyes and it was six o'clock.

I picked up a bottle of good wine on the way home and walked into the savory smell of dinner on the stove. The kids greeted me with cries of *Daddy* and my wife glanced over at me with a quiet smile. She didn't say anything. She didn't need to. The fire was burning just as hot inside her as it was me.

I love my kids. I've always enjoyed sharing meals with them. But dinner couldn't have been over soon enough. Between the two of us, we finished the bottle of wine and opened a second before it was bedtime for the children. We worked with purpose, splitting the chores that needed to be done before we could be with each other. I cleaned and cleared away dinner while Emily put the kids down for the night. My hands were practically shaking as I set the last plate into the dishwasher. That was when my cell phone chimed. A text.

–I left a gift at the bottom of the stairs. text me when you get it.

There, on the third step of our carpet-lined stairwell, was the purse camera's receiver. I smiled, sending the reply immediately. I flipped it on and a surprisingly high resolution picture of our bedroom filled the little screen. A moment later, Emily stepped before it, smiling demurely. She wore her short red kimono, which didn't quite cover the red garter strap that snapped to the lacy top of her stocking.

"Can you hear me?" she asked with a smile, fingering the silky belt that was loosely tied high on her waist. She held up her phone. I took the hint, texting her that I could probably hear her better if she took off her robe.

It buzzed in her hand and she looked down at it, laughing out loud. "I figured we should test it out before tomorrow."

Tomorrow. My heart shuddered.

She said, "Why don't you go into the study and get comfortable?"

With that, she tossed away her camera and unbelted her kimono.

I nearly ran into the doorjamb as I navigated through the quiet house without taking my eyes off the receiver. The garter strap led to a blood red bustier that I'd never seen before. The plunging neckline did sinful things to her breasts and just like that, my girl-next-door wife was taken from me.

"I got this a couple months ago," she explained, running her fingernails—which I noticed she'd painted red to match—over the lacy ribbing. "But I didn't have the nerve to put it on in front of you..." She laughed. "I guess I'm still not technically in front of you."

I closed the door to our study and threw myself into my desk chair as Emily crawled onto the bed. The lighting wasn't all the way up, but there was still plenty of illumination to cast shadows across her curves.

"How's the picture?" She settled onto her haunches, kneeling before me and running her hands up her body. She collected her tits in her hands, squeezing them. "Good, I hope?"

I nodded to myself. The picture was really good. Good enough that I could make out her nipples through the lace.

More incredible than the quality of the image was my wife. Or the woman who possessed her lush body. The woman vamping it up for the camera couldn't have been the woman I'd known for years, or the mother of my children. As I watched her walk the fingers of her right hand down her body and slide them into the front of her matching red thong, this brunette became fully detached from my Emily.

And yet, the hottest thing was realizing that she was the same.

"You like watching?" she asked huskily. I zeroed in on her fingers moving beneath the lace. There was no doubt at what she was doing. I didn't need to see the penetration to know it was happening. She bit her lip and groaned, undulating her hips. She rocked forward, offering her spilling cleavage to the camera, and set her free hand out before her. "I like you watching."

She lifted her hips and bowed her back until I could see the thong plunging between her buttocks. Her right hand never left her sex. Never stopped touching and twisting and driving her closer to release. The mic in the purse picked all of it up. The moans. The heavy sighs. Even the crunch of the comforter beneath her shivering body.

Emily was slow to rise, laying prone on the mattress for a long exhale. When she did raise her face to the camera, the hair around her brow had grown damp and matted. She took a deep breath and reclined into the pillows at the head of the bed.

"Well, I think we've done enough testing, don't you?" Lifting her hips up, she peeled her panties over her hips and down her stocking-clad legs.

"Jesus, Emily," I whispered to myself, feeling her name catch in my throat. Something had awoken in her and I got the feeling that it wasn't going to return to its slumber for a long, long time. She spread her legs, drawing my eyes to the still unfamiliar sight of her smooth shaven mound. I fought for air, breathing through flaring nostrils as Emily covered the slick skin with her hand.

"I hope you're on your way."

When I made it to the bedroom, she was arched and writhing against her dancing fingers. I'd already left my shirt somewhere on the stairs and by the time my knees made contact with the bed, my pants were down around my ankles.

"Oh, Ian!" Emily cried as I covered her slippery fingers with my own. She acquiesced to my touch, her body tightening as I slid two fingers inside. I covered her mouth with my own, but she was already too far gone. Too loose and jumbled to kiss and moan at the same time. She tossed her head back as my fingers worked her clit. "Stop teasing me!"

I licked the salt from her neck before replacing my hand with my cock, ramming it into her depths in one fluid motion. She grabbed the back of my head and squeezed. The pain across my scalp fueled the frenzy. I nipped at her lobe as I pounded harder, driving her to the brink before drawing back.

She began to moan in protest when I cut her off, flipping her over forcefully. Snapping her hips back against my pelvis, I thrust forward wildly, missing. My cock glanced off her clit, flopping wetly across her bare rise. Emily cried out, swiftly reaching between her thighs and making sure my next thrust found its mark.

She moaned, keeping her fingers hovering around our union. She slithered the pads of her fingertips against her clit. I could feel the vibrations of her tapping fingers as I fucked her.

I spread my fingers out along her lower back. She was making too much noise. The kids would wake. I rocked forward, angling her harder into the stacked pillows at her face. "Fuck me! Fuck me!"

I shifted behind her, pulling a knee up against my chest. My toes found purchase on the comforter, letting me push forward and drive harder. Her cries encouraged me to ignore the burn in my thighs and calves. To push higher, faster.

She thrashed about, crying, moaning. Too loud. Too uncontrolled. I twisted her mane of damp hair around my wrist and pushed her face into the pillow, muffling her cries. She struggled but I held her fast, racing to my own finish before I suffocated her.

"Gah, Em! Fuck!" I grunted.

I put everything into that final shove, feeling my balls knock against her slippery mound. They exploded, fire emptying from deep within, pouring out into Emily's tender depths. I collapsed forward, useless, as my wife finally came up for air, breathing in loud gasps.

"Are you trying to kill me?" Her face was red and breathless.

"I didn't want you to wake the kids," I said sheepishly. When I reached out to push some hair from her face, I half-expected her to shove me away. When she didn't, I took that as a good sign.

"Was I loud?" She giggled. My laughter joined hers and soon, we were in hysterics. "I love you," she said when we'd settled back down.

"I love you, too. These last few weeks have been—"

"Shhh... not tonight, honey," she whispered, kissing me softly on the lips. "Just leave it. We'll have enough time tomorrow to think all about that."

And with that, tired and worn out, we fell asleep in each other's arms.

CHAPTER 14

I didn't sleep well that night. One moment, I was tossing and turning in my own sweat. The next, the morning light was slanting across my eyes. I was alone in bed, although Emily's spot beside me was still warm. I blinked, sorting the waking life from my dreams. I heard the shower, although not the usual sounds of my wife humming as she washed herself.

My body ached from last night, but it was an ache I was slowly getting used to. I drew myself out of bed and skulked into the bathroom. I rubbed the last crusts of sleep away and Emily's hazy body materialized through the milky translucence of our shower curtain.

"Good morning," I whispered as I joined her. She looked up at me timidly, returning the greeting with a quiet voice. A shy one. She made room beneath the spray and I took it.

I wrapped my arms around her, squeezing her as the hot water explored the new pathways created by our union. She felt good in my arms. Real. I needed that reassurance. I needed something substantial to banish the ghosts of my subconscious. When I pulled back and looked at her, she could only meet my eyes for a moment. Something was on her mind. Hesitation? Fear? I kissed her lovingly, the deep caress filled with tender emotion. It was sweet. A different kind of kiss than the volcanic ones we'd been sharing these past few days.

I released her lips and dribbled kisses across her cheek, up to her ear.

"I love you," I whispered, smoothing her dark hair back across her scalp. She shivered when I kissed behind her earlobe and down the side of her neck.

I reached for her shampoo, squeezing it into my palm. She watched me brightly as I massaged it into her scalp, closing her eyes only when the suds detached themselves from her brow and swept down her face. She rinsed her hair out and handed me her loofah, turning her back to me.

We didn't speak at all. We didn't need to. We both knew what was on the other's mind. Today was the day. Today, this sweet creature before me was finally going to give herself to another man.

I soaped up her breasts before hanging the loofah up. Capturing the soft orbs in my hands, I squeezed them, feeling their weight. Her nipples tightened as I rolled them with my fingers; they were as hard as my cock pushing between her soapy buttocks. I kissed the back of her neck, tasting her fruity body soap.

Emily moaned, breaking the silence with a soft moan. "Ian, mmm..."

I didn't stop. I knew exactly how she liked her nipples played with. Would Ray? Emily swooned in my arms, reaching behind her and taking hold of my cock. I dropped one hand across her flat stomach, resting it over her smooth cleft. Despite the rush of the water, she opened up easily, hot and slick.

"Yesss..." she hissed.

"Got to make sure everything's clean," I whispered, stroking her one last time before fading back.

Emily slumped a little without my support. I turned her around and kissed her again, harder than before, but just as loving. This time, when my kisses started running away from her lips, they took a downward trajectory. Along her neck. Her clavicle. The swell of her breasts. I captured a nipple in my mouth, swirling the rigid nub with my tongue before moving on.

Emily tucked herself into the corner of the shower by the time I was on my knees. She lifted a leg onto the side of the tub, giving me access, and I nuzzled between her thighs. I glanced along the rolling landscape of her body and smiled. Pulling back, Emily gave me a questioning look before realizing what I was doing.

"May I?"

She nodded.

The shaving turned to foam as I rubbed my hands together. I rubbed it across her smooth rise and coated the petals of her pussy lips. She gasped as I grazed her clit and pulled the sensitive skin taut.

I ran the safety razor across her mound in short, teasing strokes. She plastered herself against the tiled wall, splaying her fingers for support. I lost myself in my work. The sound of the water almost drowned out her gasps. Almost. When I was through and she was smooth and glistening, I ran my tongue across the surface, tasting the bite of the shaving gel. I didn't want to miss a spot.

Emily came through her teeth, fighting to stay quiet with the kids just downstairs. The hissing sound spurred me on. I attacked her pussy. Her lips. Her swollen button. I pulled her out from the wall, letting the shower spray alight across her sex. Without hair, her clit stood exposed.

"Thank you…" she said, her breathing short and shallow. She swept her hand between her legs, a smile curling at the corners of her lips. "I take it you approve of the look?"

"I do."

I covered her mouth with mine and slid my arms down her back. I knew every detail of this woman, from the mole just off the center of her back to the way her skin dimpled just above her buttocks.

"I love it," I whispered, lifting her up and stepping into her.

She moaned as I entered her. She held my shoulders and lifted up on her tip toes to help, but I didn't need it. I knew how she wanted it before even she did. I knew when she wanted to be fucked—and over the past few days, I'd learned exactly how she liked to be fucked.

More importantly, I knew when she wanted to be loved. I'd been learning how to do that all our lives.

As I held her close and rocked her under the heat of the shower, it was love we were making. Nothing harder. Nothing softer. And certainly nothing routine. We'd come nearly full circle now. I rolled my head against hers, kissing her eye lids, her face. Her lips. She came with a quiet gasp, pulling away from me for a moment. Long enough for me to watch her rapturous face. Then I joined her, spilling my seed deep inside.

"I love you, honey," I whispered.

Emily returned the smile, but before she could return the sentiment, our kids finally made their loud and boisterous entrance.

"Mommy! Daddy! I need to PEEEEE!"

Davy at the door, shattering through our adult adventure. Emily's breath caught. I drew back, wondering if I'd remembered to lock the door. A second later, Davy proved that I hadn't.

"I need to pee, pee, pee!" he squealed. I popped my head out as I watched him slam the porcelain lid back and hop onto the seat. We'd just started potty training him and we'd been using our bathroom to do it. Now I wished I'd listened to Emily when she'd suggested the downstairs half-bath.

"You look funny, daddy!" Davy blurted, seeing only my head

around the shower curtain.

I retreated. When I looked at Emily, we broke out in hysterics.

"What's everyone doing in here?" Jenny accused. How fitting to go from tender sex to quality family time in the master bath. I grabbed us towels and we stepped out to begin one of the craziest days of our lives.

CHAPTER 15

By the time I dropped the kids off at my parents around two, I couldn't stop shaking. My mom told me not to work so hard—my excuse for needing them to watch Jenny and Davy overnight—my dad gave me a man-hug and an understanding nod—little did he know—and I was back out on the road, although I had nowhere to go. I still hadn't received the text and it was killing me.

I ended up pulling into a bar a few miles from Ray's apartment complex and having a drink. I made sure to set my phone on the bar top so I'd see the moment Emily's message arrived, although that didn't stop me from checking it anyway on the off-chance that it hadn't chimed.

That's when the fear started to set in. The insecurities. I had underestimated my wife's coworker from the moment I'd walked into Bar 88. And I'd underestimated the seriousness of this game we were playing. But that game was over, right? Ray had said it yesterday afternoon. And after today, it would finally be what it was: a fling.

Is that what I wanted? The rational part of me thought of my wife and kids, of the home we had and the love we shared, and said, *Fuck no*. But even still, a tiny part of my brain suggested that this fling was just that, a fling. Ray would leave, it would end, and Emily and I would be left with some memories of the time we were so bad. And it wasn't all bad. The sex hadn't been this good in years—if ever.

"Hey buddy, want another?" the bartender asked, breaking me out of my musings just as my phone buzzed. I glanced down at it, my heart in my throat, and shook my head.

"Just the check."

–we're hitting the pool. show time.

Butterflies roiled in my stomach. I let the wave of nausea pass, but could still feel it fluttering there, alive and needy.

I parked in the lot behind the pool and pulled out the monitor. In the daylight, the trees that I'd hidden in earlier that week looked so much thinner, and despite the heat of this September afternoon, the leaves were already beginning to turn. No chance hiding in there.

Luckily, the lot was much more full today and it was fairly easy to blend in. I just hoped no one came out and saw me sitting like a creep in the car.

I flipped on the seven-inch receiver and was instantly treated with a wide angle view of the pool. Emily was there, dressed in her dark polka-dot two-piece, busy slathering sunscreen on her pale skin. For a moment, however, I didn't see her as my wife. I saw her like the guys around her saw her: an athletic brunette with nice curves and a pretty face. I realized that I wasn't the only one watching, especially when she bent forward to do her legs. Her cleavage poured out of the haltered top, her breasts glistened with sunblock and sweat. She was wearing her oversized faux-designer sunglasses and I wondered if she knew what she was doing to her audience. The tiny smile on her mouth suggested she might.

"Emily is just his type," a blonde standing in the foreground said, close enough to the mic of our hidden purse cam. Younger than my wife, her bikini pushed the limits a little more—not that I was complaining. Bright pink, the twisted bandeau style top made her full, golden breasts look fantastic. The haltered string around her neck barely held them in check.

She went on. "Pretty, petite, and a little older. Do you really think they're just co-workers?"

"That's what he says," the man she was talking to replied. He was a sandy-haired version of Ray, although maybe a little taller. He was being very diplomatic, but I got the feeling he was tip-toeing around the young hottie.

"You saw the way he greeted her at the door." My stomach turned over. Until now, this game had only involved three people: me, Emily, and an unwitting Ray. I preferred it that way. Easier to contain. Easier to control. But then, control was what I was losing with each passing day, wasn't it?

"She's married," the guy replied, drawing a laugh from the blonde.

"When has that ever stopped Ray? I think he might even prefer that. Come on, Brian, you must know something."

"I know that everyone here's a consenting adult and it's not my place to make judgments."

"But you think she's hot, too," the girl said testily.

"Yes, she's very MILFy, but you're all I need, baby," the guy—Brian—said, kissing her even as she rolled her eyes.

They joined Emily and Ray by the pool, and before I had a chance to wrap my head around what I'd just heard, Brian and Ray were tossing a squealing Emily into the pool. The blonde quickly followed. The four of them goofed around in the pool, looking very much like two couples. It was an incredible thing to witness. I watched Emily smile and laugh. I watched her really enjoy herself. And most haunting of all, I watched how she looked at Ray.

She had maintained that she was doing this for me. She might believe that, but all I had to do was look at her to know that she was lying to herself. Another reminder that the longer this went on, the harder it would be to stop.

They weren't the only ones occupying the pool, so the hanky panky was kept to a minimum—although Brian and his girlfriend seemed to stretch the boundaries of what was decent. Ray and Emily were much more restrained—on the surface, anyway.

At one point, when he had her up against the side of the pool, I got the feeling that their hands weren't just holding each other for support. She had her head tipped back and was laughing, too far from the mics for me to hear. Ray lifted a hand from the water to touch her neck and stroke her jaw with his thumb. She looked at him and they started kissing, soft and sweet. Before it went further, she lifted herself out of the pool and crossed the deck to where the camera was sitting. Ray didn't follow immediately, choosing to watch the sway of her buttocks in her wet bikini.

Emily winked before reaching out and flipping off the camera.

•••

The receiver didn't pick up a thing for another hour, although it was only fifteen minutes before Ray's friends left the pool, still tangled in each other's arms.

As I sat in the car and waited, a conversation I'd shared with Ray a long time ago returned to me.

...she's been in a relationship so long that maybe she's forgotten what getting all hot and heavy is like. All women like to be swept off their feet, you know, get caught up in the moment and throw caution to the wind...

...has she thrown caution to the wind?

...not yet, but I think I see it there, the gleam in her eye, that she *wants to. Maybe she just needs a little push...*

I'd given her a lot more than a push and Ray had done a hell of a lot more than sweep her off her feet. As I watched Emily and Ray cross the parking lot to his apartment, hand-in-hand, it was hard to fathom how we got from that conversation to this moment.

Another agonizing twenty minutes passed. I drove the car closer to his unit and fidgeted with the receiver. Was I in range? Had she remembered to turn it on? Had they started and something was malfunctioning? I nearly called Emily just to check.

I got out of the car and started marching toward Ray's garden style apartment, my mind working overtime trying to figure out some excuse I could use for being so close. I rounded a corner and nearly ran into Brian and his girlfriend on their way out.

"I'm... sorry..." I stuttered as the tall guy grabbed me and kept me on my feet.

Our eyes met and for a split second I thought I was busted.

"Better watch where you're going," he said, clapping me on the shoulder. "Take care."

Of course he didn't recognize me. But Ray would. And this was all a little too dangerous for me. I skulked back to the car and was situating myself back into the driver's side seat when my phone came to life. I picked it up on the first ring.

"Hey, what's going on?"

"We're just about ready. Are you here?" Her voice was low. I could hear running water in the background.

We're just about ready. *We.*

"I have been. Who was that blonde by the pool?"

"That was Ashleigh, his friend's girlfriend. Don't get too excited, dear. They left, so there will be no threesome."

"A guy can dream, can't he?"

"Anyway, I have to go. I just wanted to make sure you're ready. I'm going to rinse the chlorine off. Then it's show time."

I swallowed hard. I was glad she couldn't see my face. See the anxiety that was all over it. "Great."

"You still want this?"

"I do." And I did. I *so* did.

"Okay. Gotta go."

And she hung up.

Another fifteen minutes of waiting. This time, I knew it wasn't a technical mishap. It was Emily getting ready—getting ready for another man for the sole purpose of going to bed with him. Was I still okay with that? Did I really want that?

The circumstances weren't ideal. I looked around at the cramped space of my car. At the tiny receiver that I held in my hands. I didn't like that I couldn't be closer. That I couldn't look into her eyes and know that she saw me back. But still, the answer was the same as before. I did. Just this one time, I did.

The screen came alive at last. The camera was somehow positioned at the head of Ray's queen-sized bed, covered in maroon red sheets and matching pillows. No pictures adorned the walls, although the quality was sharp enough that I could see the dusty rectangles where they once hung. To the side of the bed was Emily wearing just the purple bra and panty set I'd seen a few nights back.

After all the fiddling I'd done with the receiver device, I'd discovered a few things. Like how it could record. I made sure it started recording now. Didn't want to miss this.

Ray entered the room, completely naked.

All women want to be swept off their feet...

And this was the exact kind of guy who usually did it.

I wasn't attracted to him, but I could imagine what Emily must have appreciated. We hadn't talked much about Ray specifically. The game had always been more abstract, played on a level of theory and emotion. Part of Ray's appeal was obvious: the muscles, the broad shoulders, his thick cock. But I began to wonder what else Emily was attracted to.

She sauntered up to him, drawing my eyes back to her and the way her ass moved in her thong. She kissed him swiftly, rubbing herself against him before pulling back and taking his hand. Ray grinned and let himself be positioned in the middle of the bed.

"Why aren't I surprised you like to take the lead in bed?" he asked as Emily crawled up between his legs.

"I just want to show you just how much I want you, and how sorry I am for keeping you waiting. Tonight, I'm yours, baby. You can have me however you want me."

The words slowly sank in as Emily took Ray into her mouth, teasing his cock. She was his tonight. More than that, she gladly gave herself to him.

"Emily..." Ray gasped as she swirled the crown of his dick around with her tongue. Her hazel eyes were locked onto his, saying to him wordlessly how much she enjoyed doing this. How much she loved sucking him off. Christ knew how many times she'd done it in the past couple weeks.

She tongued down his shaft when he looked ready to blow. Holding it against his hard abs, she sucked his balls into her mouth. Her eyes shifted. She stared up at the camera. Right at me. *Is this what you want?* she seemed to ask. I nodded, despite knowing that she couldn't see me. Perspiration was building, causing her bangs to stick to her forehead.

Tearing her eyes away, she dove back onto his cock. Ray helped us both out, holding her hair from her face so we could watch her as she worked. Her cheeks hollowed. Ray began lifting his hips to meet her, moaning her name. Moaning how good she felt. He came and she swallowed, sucking him until he had nothing left to give.

"I love making you cum." She crawled across his muscular body, covering him with her own. The words stung. She *loved* it. I reminded myself that this was a one-time thing—the last time—but a cynical side of me wondered how realistic that was. Could she give it up like that? Cold turkey?

"And you do it so well. I should return the favor."

Emily was giddy as she was kissed and turned onto her back. He trailed kisses down her neck and out her shoulder, pulling the bra straps down. "You look good in purple, but I bet you'll look even better out of it."

I rolled my eyes, but Emily seemed to eat it up.

"Ray..."She moaned as he nipped at her nipple through the lace of the bra. "Oh, baby…"

He torture-teased her, alternating breasts and sensitive nipples without peeling the bra the rest of the way off. She cried out with a harshness that made me wonder how hard he was nibbling on her.

He laughed. "You love to tease me so much, I think I should return the favor."

"God, don't stop, Ray…"

At last, the bra came away and he attacked with his tongue. Emily jerked liked a marionette in the hands of a drunk puppeteer. She arched her back, filling his mouth with her nipples. Ray held her lithe body close, sliding an arm behind her back. The other sought her pussy.

"Please... please..." Emily begged. She dug her fingers into his shoulders. He didn't relent.

Ray pinned her hands to the bed above her with one arm. She

twisted under his mouth as he continued to maul her hyper-sensitive breasts. I knew what he was doing. I'd done it before, knew how much she hated it. He was bringing her to the very edge of orgasm, holding her there as long as she could stand, then retreating before she fell off it.

"Please...please...take me...Ray..." She was so ready for it, the evidence shiny and wet as he pulled off her panties. She clawed at him, trying to pull him on top of her, but Ray was too strong. He pulled out of her grasp and sank down between her thighs, spreading them open.

After all the teasing, Ray finally went for the throat. Slurping her clit into his mouth, she grabbed the pillow behind her head, mashed it in her hands, and rammed her hips up off the bed, grinding into Ray's face. She screamed.

Emily was a goddess. My goddess. I'd never seen her look so wanton, but the image would burn in my mind forever. Seeing her inner animal unleashed while I was with her was one thing. Seeing it with Ray was out-of-body. It wasn't any better or sexier, it was just different. So profoundly different.

Ray brought her to the edge of a second orgasm before drawing back. He was breathing heavily, his head slumped between his hulking shoulders, his eyes glancing up at her like a panther. "I guess you've waited long enough," he growled, prowling over her prone body.

"I want you, baby. I want you so much," Emily cooed, kissing his face and neck. I thought back to that first night that I'd met Ray, coming home drunk and imagining it was Ray fucking her when I had. Soon, I wouldn't have to imagine. This was the fruition of all those fantasies. Was I ready for it?

"Tell me what you want, Em. Say it."

"I want you to fuck me."

Jealousy speared through my body. My heart was beating fast enough that I thought I might have a heart attack if I didn't calm myself. But I didn't want to fucking calm myself!

"I want your cock," she said. She reached for him, wrapping her hand around his saliva-bathed shaft.

My own cock surged. I no longer needed to pretend she was talking about Ray. She *was* fucking talking about Ray! I could hardly breathe. That little monitor shook in my hand.

"Then take it." He held up a condom wrapper. "Put it inside you, baby."

The mic of the purse was good enough to pick up the wet tear as Emily opened the condom. She was smiling up at him the whole time, chewing on her lip at their shared mischief. I was shut out of this moment.

And I was okay with that. The bright look on Emily's face made it all worth it.

Emily's hands shook as she rolled the latex down Ray's thickness.

I stopped breathing. This was the moment of truth. I felt crushed by contradiction. Jealousy like battery acid; arousal like electricity. I wanted her to push him away, to deny him, and at the same time that I wanted her to be taken. Hard.

The camera gave the perfect vantage between their slick bodies. Fate was in our favor. I watched as Emily positioned the fat head against her swollen lips, splitting her open. I drew breath into already packed lungs. Ray pushed her hand aside and lunged forward.

"AH!" Emily cried, her voice cutting off as he buried herself inside him in one quick thrust.

I jerked in my car, nearly cumming. Nearly joining my wife in what looked like an exquisite orgasm. I forced my hand off my cock—I hadn't even realized I'd started rubbing myself—forced myself to breathe. My nostrils flared. On the screen in my hand, Ray had pinned Emily's arms above her head once again and was fucking her slowly. He'd pull back with patient precision, and then he'd lunge forward, sending a stiffening jolt through Emily's body.

These two were now lovers. The deep stares they shared left no doubt about that. Emily was my wife and the mother of my children, we were in love and this didn't change that. I could analyze this relationship rationally. This had started as a game that I'd created, and while I knew she wasn't doing it just for me, I did play a big role in her motivations.

Yet it was impossible to stop the very irrational feelings of betrayal. They were like weeds in a garden. Inevitable. I watched as they stared into one another's eyes and realized that Emily and Ray had developed a bond that I would never be a part of. It was like a dark cloud had descended around me, buzzing with deadly lightning.

"I've wanted to fuck you for so long, Em," Ray grunted. "I've thought about this so many times."

"Uhn… Ray…"

"The way you teased around the office, I knew you were fucking hot for it. I knew you needed more than you were getting."

Was that it? Did she not get enough from me? Was that why she'd started wearing sexier lingerie, started getting back into shape? Was this affair an inevitability? The dark cloud thickened.

"Ray…"

Part of me wanted her to deny it—to correct him. But all she did was moan as Ray's hips began to fuck her faster.

"And then you started fucking teasing me… you wouldn't give it up, but I knew you wanted it…"

Was this because of me? Was this where I came in? Or had this all begun before I even entered the picture. The insecurities swarmed.

"Fuck, you feel good..." he said. "God, you're a fucking great cocksucker, but I had to fuck you, Em."

How many blow jobs had she given? How many times had she swallowed his cum?

"Fuck me!" Emily cried out as his slow and methodical tease gave way to the pounding she really wanted. She wrapped her legs around his torso, humping up into his as she screamed out another orgasm.

Ray pulled out before she was done, flipping her over and yanking her hips hard, pulling her ass into the air. He rammed back into her as she rode out the last throes of her climax, growling at how fucking good her ass looked. Emily clawed the sheets as he jackhammered her.

"Fuck me, fuck me!" Her cries came desperate, even through the muffling sheets.

He spanked her, each slap drawing a yelping moan from Emily. We'd never done that before. I'd never been so rough. Emily kept cumming, rolling through her orgasms one after another.

At last, Ray released her from his grip and she collapsed forward in a sweaty heap. He rolled onto the bed next to her, kissing her as she recovered. This was usually the part of the night when she shut off the light and we went to bed, energy sapped and bodies sated. But Ray wasn't sated. His condom-sheathed erection was a presence between them, and Emily surprised me when she reached between them and wrapped her hand around it. Their kisses grew heated. Ray's hands explored once again, finding her tits, her pussy. I watched as he curled two fingers along the clean shaven rise and pushed them into her.

I was discreetly rubbing myself through my pants, but was starting to think that maybe I should relocate from Ray's parking lot, where anyone could walk by. I hadn't planned this far in advance. Hell, I hadn't planned any of this. I think that a very large part of me never thought it would come to this, even as I drove over here—that this was all some kind of elaborate bluff, a way for Emily to teach me a lesson.

"Ah, yeah, fuck me, Em!" Ray grunted as my wife pushed her young stud flat onto his back and mounted him. "Ride it."

He slid his hands up her hips and over her breasts, pulling and teasing her nipples. It drove Emily crazy.

"Ohhh… baby…I love your cock…"

Her words stung, but I loved hearing them.

"I love fucking you…Ray…"

Was that for me? Or for her?

"I'm gonna fuck you all night."

I shifted nervously, checking the battery life on the receiver. It looked about half-charged. All night wasn't part of what we'd discussed, but—

"Yes…yes!"

—but we hadn't discussed much at all. I'd been too afraid to talk specifics, and now I was left with a confused jumble of expectations.

Then Emily looked up at the camera. Up at me. *I'm fucking him, I'm FUCKING HIM!*

Her face shifted like smoke moments before combustion: one moment triumphant, the next challenging, the next engulfed in desire so hot my eyes watered. I felt her, like she was right in front of me. I touched the screen. I couldn't be there, but in a way she was right: I *was* there.

Ray slid his hands back down to her hips, taking control of her. I watched his thick arms flex as he lifted her up and slammed her back down. She was a sex toy that he was about to get off on. "Uh! Uh! UHHH!" she grunted, folding forward.

"Emily!" Ray cried, yanking her against his hips one final time.

He thrust forward, his whole body leaving the mattress and taking Emily with him as though she weighed no more than a feather. She gripped the headboard, her legs hanging off him. Her face filled the camera.

"I'm cumming!" Ray groaned, his voice drowned out only by Emily's throaty cry.

Reality snapped into focus. *My* reality. I'd been in the room with them. I'd been part of the scene. Now, I'd been jerked back to the front seat of the car, steering wheel jammed into my knee, my cock quivering in my pants.

"Baby, that was so good," Emily cooed on the recording. It felt tinny and two-dimensional. I felt alone.

I also felt like I had to go find some more privacy. I set the hand-held receiver down and switched the car on.

CHAPTER 16

My mind always wandered when I was alone and out for a drive. Even as supercharged as it was now, this was no different.

I thought about our life since Ray had entered it, the last few days in particular. Emily and I had been friends and lovers so long that we'd grown comfortable. We'd become efficient with one another. I knew how to get her off quickly; she knew precisely what I liked. If it ain't broke, don't fix it, right? And yet, things were more broken than either of us had realized.

Emily *had* started dressing more sexy. She *had* started going to the gym again. And I'd learned through Ray that she'd even flirted with her coworkers—at least when she was loosened up enough. She wasn't having an affair—she probably never would, but that didn't mean that the thought wasn't there.

The thought of Emily having an affair shook me to the core, yet in light of what I'd just witnessed—what I was still witnessing—I wondered how I really felt about it. In the last two weeks, I'd set Ray and Emily up and pushed her into sleeping with him. It didn't matter that she wanted it now. That didn't change the fact that obsession had driven me to crave this.

If I hadn't arranged it—if it had happened naturally between the two of them—was it any different?

Of course it was. If she'd slept with Ray without me knowing, I wouldn't have been part of it. I wouldn't have been in those bushes by the pool, or on the phone during their car ride, or here now, monitor in my hands.

I scanned the neighborhood. A strip mall backed up against the apartment complex, the parking lot completely empty. I pulled into there. Empty store fronts stared at me as I drove by.

Emily had been so hot with Ray. She reconnected with a part of her sexuality that had laid dormant for years. That I was there was important to her—to both of us—but it wasn't necessary.

"...don't think we're done... do you...?" Their voices tuned in and out like a radio station losing its signal as I drove along the boundaries of the camera's range. "...no, but... glass of water... you like something...?"

I pulled around the back of the strip mall, cruising by the shuttered doors of the loading docks. I sought out what I thought was Ray's apartment—curtains drawn but lights on—and parked as close as I could get.

Heat licked along the back of my neck. There—that's where it had all happened. Where we'd risked years of happy marriage because of an obsession that had consumed me.

But it was over now, wasn't it? They'd done their thing. They'd... had sex. The game was over. I could finally put my obsession to rest.

And yet there was no way I was leaving.

This wasn't about me and my fantasy anymore. It had taken on a new and dangerous life of its own—a danger I saw in the way Emily and Ray looked at each other.

I shut off the car and picked up my monitor once again. Ray was alone in the bedroom, the thin flat sheet covering him. He had his iPhone out, surfing or texting or tweeting about all the fucking, who knows.

I checked my phone to make sure that Emily hadn't called. Maybe she used the glass of water excuse to sneak out and come home? My hope, if that was what it was, was short-lived. No message.

Before I even set it down, the door swung open and my brain detached itself from reality.

At first, I didn't understand what I was seeing. Ray's friend, Brian, was there, sandy-haired and built like a Billabong ad. That couldn't have been Emily in his arms, though, wearing nothing but one of Ray's white Oxfords.

Brian couldn't still be there. I'd passed him on the stairs, the fear of discovery still fresh. I sat back enough for the bucket seat to creak and groan, running my fingers through my hair. Trying to come to grips with the situation.

Ray spoke as my mind whirred. "I was wondering where you were. Guess you ran into some*one* rather than some*thing*."

"He was just out there, I didn't..." Emily hesitated. Her eyes wavered between Ray and the camera. I felt the snap of connection through the screen again. She was as shocked by the turn of events as I was.

"It's cool. As long as I get you to myself most of the night, I don't mind sharing with an old friend for a while. I told you he wanted you, too." Ray laughed.

Brian said, "See, I told you he wouldn't mind. And he's right, Ray's got great taste in women."

"You boys are talking like I have no say in this..."

The two guys shared a look as Brian set her down. So this wasn't the first time they'd shared a woman before. A gulp caught in my throat, growing tighter when Ray gave a quick nod that I wasn't sure

Emily even saw.

Brian swept her hair away and kissed her neck from behind. She didn't stop him. Instead, she leaned her head to the side, exposing her neck. He exposed even more as he pushed the Oxford shirt off her shoulders. It pooled around her ankles.

I gasped. Emily gasped. He traced the contours of her nudity, palming her breasts before settling over her bare shaven mound. Emily moaned, arching her back and rising up onto the balls of her feet as he pushed his fingers inside her.

Ray crawled across the bed to join them, rising to full height. He was still naked, his thickening cock swinging between his thighs as he stepped up against Emily and pushed his tongue down her throat. He didn't linger long before shifting to her nipples.

The guys manipulated her body until she was in a fog, showering her in kisses, touches, reducing her to a quivering collection of senses. Brian stripped as the three of them poured onto the bed. Emily was still squeezed between them, although I wasn't sure she was able to distinguish one man from the next. She twisted between them, moaning and sighing, drowning in the sea of masculinity.

Again, I sat there, watching the whole thing in disbelief. Emily? My Emily? Was she really doing this? Did she really just reach out and begin jerking the two men off simultaneously?

Ray and Brian attacked her breasts together, a mouth on each, their hands working in together between her legs. She had no chance. She came fast and hard, and when Brian pushed his cum-coated fingers into her mouth, Emily sucked them greedily.

When she slumped away from their sweaty bodies, her hair was a damp and sexy mess. She pushed it out of her face, still breathing hard. "What am I going to do with these two strong young cocks?"

She could barely get the words out in one breath.

My jaw hit the floor. Any reluctance that she may have had was gone. She wanted this—wanted a threesome with two virile young guys who were not me. She looked at the camera one last moment—whether with worry or challenge or simple exhibition, I'll never know—and then slithered down between Ray's legs.

With one hand wrapped around Brian's cock, she bobbed her head on Ray's.

"Wait 'til you get a load of this," Ray said to Brian. A moment later, Emily switched cocks.

At full strength, Brian was large enough to prove a challenge for Emily to swallow whole. She took what she could, though, and jerked off what she couldn't. And as she dipped along Brian's impressive manhood and held his eyes the whole time, I realized that she was performing for him. For all of us. And she was reveling in it.

Before Brian could get comfortable, she slurped free and switched to Ray—although she kept her hand on the blonde, polishing the saliva-slickened head of his member. Back and forth, she took care of both men like she did this all the time.

Finally, when she had them both on edge, she stopped and sat back. Her smile stretched from ear to ear. "How are we going to do this, guys?"

I tightened the grip I had of my cock and watched her orchestrate her first ever threesome.

"Someone can't wait to get fucked," Ray chuckled.

"You're right," Emily said. Again, a lightning fast glance at the camera. "Less talking, more screwing."

"I hate to leave a pretty lady waiting," Brian said. Ray tossed him a condom packet and he laid back, deftly fitting the latex over his large cock.

My heart skipped, despite the fact that we'd already been here with Ray earlier this evening. With Ray, I'd had time to anticipate. He was a known quantity. Brian was new—new and *large*. My breath caught as he pulled my wife up onto his lap and held his cock up for her. Emily licked her lips, her eyes fluttering shut as she sank to the hilt.

She gasped, allowing a moan to escape, twisted and high-pitched. "Oh, it feels so good."

With her back mostly to me, I couldn't see much—a flash of his cock between her thighs as she rose, his balls nestling between her thighs as she fell—but it was enough.

He palmed her tits at first, but as they began to really go for it, he slid them around to her buttocks and took control. He thrust up each time she dropped on him, grinding together until Emily was screaming for him to fuck her. "Goddam, your fucking pussy is tight."

Like me, Ray was stroking his cock as he watched, pacing himself. Unlike me, he was able to join the action. I watched him tear open a new condom and slip it on.

"You're a fucking little slut, aren't you?" Brian asked. He left hand prints on her plush ass.

"Yes...yes..." She was so into this. So ready and willing to accept her role for them. "I'm a fucking slut for you guys..."

Ray looked at Brian and the two guys shared a nod that Emily didn't see. A moment later, Ray pulled her off his friend. She whined in frustration, although was no match for Ray as he rolled her onto her back, grabbed her hips, and hoisted her up to him.

With just her head and shoulders resting on the mattress, Emily took the hint. She quickly placed his cock against her dewy petals. Their eyes met, sharing that frightening closeness. He sank in without resistance.

Emily grabbed her tits and squeezed them harder than I ever

dared to as Ray took her. Brian snapped off his condom and knelt beside her, rubbing his cock against her lips. Enthusiastically, she wrapped her mouth around it and sucked. This was now officially a threesome.

If she was capable of this, what else was she capable of doing? What had I unlocked in her?

Neither guy was particularly gentle. The double manhandling continued. Brian and Ray were on a seesaw and Emily was the pivot. Brian held the back of her head and fucked her mouth as vigorously as Ray took her pussy.

My balls tightened. I was close. She no longer had eyes for the camera. Her world was filled with the cocks drilling her, filling her holes. Fucking her senseless. Her brow creased. I recognized it. Her orgasm. She was close. I jerked harder. The guys didn't let up. If anything, they sensed the kill and went for it. Ray pulled her legs up over his shoulders and pounded her hard enough that the slaps nearly drowned out their wild grunts.

"Ah! Ahhh!" Emily screamed around Brian's cock.

I came with her, sending an arc of my cum across my t-shirt. I saw stars. I rolled down the windows to suck in the fresh night air.

And when I looked at the screen, it was black.

It took me a few minutes to realize that the show was over. For me, anyway. Two hours of battery life felt so short.

I debated what to do now that I was literally out of the picture. I think I was supposed to call her, to let her know the camera had run its course, to give her a head's up that she was on her own.

That wasn't going to happen. All I had to do was close my eyes and think about the ecstasy in her face to know that the rest of the night wasn't about me.

That didn't mean I was totally okay with the twist in our little game. After being ravished by two guys as good looking as Ray and Brian, how could I compete? Yes, my mind went there, despite all of Emily's reassurances that she loved me; that she was doing this for me.

Part of it was true, sure, but there was a healthy dose of bullshit in that line. And I now had the video to prove it.

At home, I reviewed the home made porno—still in disbelief that it was my wife acting the star. The way she gave herself so readily to first Ray, then Brian, then both men, wasn't done for anyone but herself. Question was, was I okay with that?

I still didn't have a fully formed answer to when Emily finally rolled in, well past three in the morning.

CHAPTER 17

I was barely awake when I heard the door open.

I'd dozed off in the den in front of our plasma TV. The picture was frozen on the final recorded image. It wasn't HD, but the quality was sharp enough to capture the creases in Emily's forehead and around her tightly shut eyes. It captured the thick sheen of sweat on her face, and the smear of saliva across her cheek. Behind her, Ray was frozen, mid-thrust, holding her hips in a reverse wheelbarrow pose. To her side, Brian knelt, feeding his cock into her slack-jawed mouth, his fingers twisting her damp, dark locks.

"Oh..." Emily's voice was soft as she stopped just inside the arched passage that separated living room from den. I didn't say anything because I didn't know what to say.

But really, maybe that wasn't quite it. Maybe I was giving myself more credit than I deserved. Maybe that girl frozen like a porn star on my television had always been there, waiting to emerge.

"Ian." She drew me back to the present.

"Hey, hon."

"Are you okay?" She sounded scared.

"Yeah."

"Are we okay? Ian, talk to me." Panic crept into her voice.

I rubbed sleep from the corners of my eyes and looked at her at last. "You're home late."

"Sorry, I fell asleep." She forced a smile. "I was pretty worn out by the end."

I couldn't help but smile a little at that. "I can imagine."

"Ian, you're killing me. What the hell are you thinking?"

"I've got to be honest. I'm blown away. I don't know what I thought it would be like, but I wasn't expecting that."

"In a good way?" It was funny to hear her so timid after what I'd witnessed.

"Yeah, I think so." Her face went pale. I went on. "Emily, you love me, right? Still, I mean?"

She collapsed next to me on the couch, tears beginning to well up on her eyes. "Of course, baby. How could you even ask that, after..."

"Hey, hey, don't worry, Em. I love you. I'm not angry about it. I couldn't be, could I? I mean, I asked for this and it was the hottest thing I've ever seen." It took saying it aloud for me to realize it, but that felt honest. "I just didn't know it would be like that."

She relaxed a little. "Do you mean when I came back with Brian?"

"Well, yeah, obviously I wasn't expecting that, but I just meant the whole thing. When you and Ray did it...the way you just gave yourself over to it...I mean, wow...you really gave yourself over."

That wasn't it, either. I raked my fingers through my hair, searching for words.

"I thought that's what you wanted, honey. You wanted me to sleep with Ray and I don't know any other way except to just go for it."

"No, that's not..." I ground my teeth a little and took a deep breath. Finally, I'd found something to be upset about. It wasn't her fooling around with some guy from work. Or fucking him. Or even fucking his buddy. It was about the way she kept trying to peg this one all on me. The frustration diffused through me like blood in water.

"Stop telling me you only did this for me. You wanted him. I could see it in your eyes. In the way you used your body. All this week you acted like you didn't want to do this, but...I mean, come on, Em. I'm not blind!"

My wife's jaw set. She started to reply again and again, stopping herself before anything more than a broken syllable left her lips. Finally, she closed her eyes, looked away, then back.

"Yes, of course I wanted to fuck Ray. He's a hot guy. I just didn't want to hurt you, honey. I was thinking about you the whole time." She squeezed my hand.

"I know. I saw you looking. That was... that was hot. It was like we were in it together."

"We were, honey," she said, pushing her hand into my lap. I think both of us were surprised to find me hard. "It made me so wet to know you were watching me be so bad."

I couldn't deny how turned on it made me. Was I okay with that woman? And what if she grew bored with me? There was nothing left to fret about but that.

Made me so wet...

I grew as she rubbed me through my loose pajamas. A week ago, she'd never even be able to form those words. Hell, last night, I'm not sure she could have vocalized them without a few drinks in her.

"I couldn't believe what I saw."

Emily pulled at my pants and I obliged, lifting my butt off the couch. My cock sprang out and she wrapped her warm hands around it. "I can't believe it, either. It's like I was possessed."

"It was so crazy, and so fucking sexy. You're a wonder, Emily." Her hands felt good.

"So you like seeing me all crazy and sexy?" she asked, leaning over. Her hair brushed my thighs as she dipped low. I groaned, feeling her swirl the head of my cock in her mouth. She looked back up at me through her long lashes, waiting for an answer.

"I did. It was unreal." Truthfully, yes, but not honestly. I left things out. For now, it was better that way. We'd work through this. But right now...

"And you liked seeing me slutty?" She kissed my cock again, all the while keeping her eyes on me. She licked the precum from its head and savored it on her tongue.

"Yeah...Emm..." She started sucking me, teasing me with a technique that she'd refined in the last couple weeks. If nothing changed but that, I'd be a happy man. I was just terrified that too much had changed.

Grabbing the remote, I wound the recording back to the moment where Emily's two studs started teasing her. Emily must have heard herself on the television because she started blowing me harder, swallowing me to the root. I moaned. If I hadn't cum twice already, I wouldn't have lasted more than a minute. Not with the way she played with my balls as she worked me. Not with the sight of her kneeling between Ray and Brian as they passed her back and forth between them.

I needed her. I needed to show her that while guys like Brian and Ray would come and go, I'd always be there, and I'd always be enough.

"Ian..." Emily protested, but only for a moment. I pulled her against me as I groped at her skintight jeans. She wasn't going to refuse me. Not after what all she'd done tonight. She stood, unsnapped the dark denim, and eased them over her hips. She was red and sore. Used. The nice guy Ian would have given her a break. I wasn't the nice guy Ian right now.

Yanking my shirt off, I pulled her into my lap, facing away. Facing the screen. She quickly got what I was going for, crying out as I pierced her.

"Watch it, Emily. Watch yourself…it's so sexy…"

She was mesmerized by her on-screen persona. Ray lifted her into him, spreading her womanhood as Brian entered the picture from the side. We fucked slowly at first, watching the drama unfold. I pulled her tank top up over her breasts, clutching them. Squeezing them.

"Look at how you're taking it, Emily." I pinched her nipples, twisting them enough to draw a hushed cry from her. "It's like you were born for sex."

She moaned in agreement.

"Did you feel like their plaything? Did you want them to use you?" The questions welled up from somewhere deep and dark inside me, where my fears and insecurities bred in subterranean ecosystems, out of the light.

"Yes, honey. I wanted them to use me all night. I wanted you to see them use me."

"Don't tell me what I want to hear, Em. Tell me the truth." I twisted her nipples again, emphasizing my point. "There's no room for anything else anymore."

"Yes!" she cried out. On screen, her final, recorded orgasm was approaching. She was used. A fuck machine. A total slut. "Fuck me… fuck your little slut, Ian…"

"God you're a slut…such a fucking slut…"

"Yes! Yes, Ian, baby! I'm your slut. Fuck me, fuck me, Ian. Cum with me…"

The picture froze again, that last visage of passion overrun with depravity. We came watching that. Is that how this story would end? Is that what we'd be left with? A slut and a cuckold?

Emily twisted around in my arms, looking as exhausted as I felt. "Can we please go to bed now?"

I kissed her softly—the way I used to kiss her she was my wife and mother to our kids.

"Of course."

EPILOGUE

Be careful what you wish for...

I woke the next morning, exhausted yet unable to sleep. The sun had begun to rise, and I could just make out Emily's sleeping form. Her dark hair blanketed her face. Her bare shoulder rose and fell with her steady breathing.

Sleep and the dawning turned everything timeless. I saw the woman I'd first met so many years ago. And the bride on the first morning of our life as husband and wife. And the new mom, exhausted from being up with our infant son.

I touched Emily's cheek. She stirred without waking.

...you just might get it.

I'd pushed this woman to do things that neither of us thought we'd ever do—things I never knew we wanted. That was on me—Ray, Brian, the uncertain future.

Had Ray watched her like this last night, when she'd fallen asleep? The hypothetical question felt like a hot poker rammed through me. That image—Ray propped up on an arm, studying Emily as she slept—bothered me more than any other from last night.

I hugged Emily close, reminding myself that she was here with me. That I had nothing to lose.

Emily drifted out of sleep, her eyes opening just a hair.

"Morning," I said.

"Ian." A sleepy smile spread across her face. "Not right now. I'm still sore."

It took me a moment to realize what she was talking about. Hugging her close, I realized I was hard and pressed up against her hip. She thought I wanted to make love again.

I kissed her on the forehead. "Okay, honey. Go back to sleep. I'll get us breakfast."

I slipped out of bed and rooted around for jeans and a shirt. Changing in the hall, I decided to walk to the neighborhood bagel shop.

The early morning air helped clear my head of more than just sleep. I finally looked back on the last couple weeks and realized just how crazy they'd been. I'd set-up Ray with Emily, encouraged her to meet him for another night, and finally gave her the go-ahead to sleep with him. In the process, I'd witnessed a side of my wife that I'd never suspected was there.

It scared me. It excited me. It confused me. I wondered what I'd woken in her, and whether I was prepared for more.

On the one hand, the one ruled by my obsession, I wanted to see so much more. The more prudent Ian knew that it was time to put it to rest. I'd played with fire and lived. There was a lesson there.

•••

"So, about last night..." Emily began.

"Yeah...last night..." I'd come home with a bag of bagels and coffee. We still had a little time before we had to pick the kids up and needed this talk.

"Are we okay?" That question again. It was good to know she was as insecure as I was. It was something we could share and build from. I answered her as I had last night.

"You still love me?"

"Of course I do. More than ever."

"Then we're good."

Emily studied me as she chewed on her bagel. "If you have something to say, Ian, then just say it."

I'd imagined this question coming all morning and had rehearsed my response so that it would come naturally. Only now, when it was time to perform, I stumbled through the white lie. "Last night was incredible, but I don't think I can take another like it."

Emily arched her brows. "Let me get this straight. You're telling me that you enjoyed watching me act like a... well, like a complete slut last night..."

"Yes."

"That you're not mad about it..."

"I'm not." I definitely wasn't.

"That you still love me..."

"More than ever." And more importantly, lusted after her.

"And now your fantasy has been fulfilled?"

"I think so, yeah," I said. But not really. That was the nugget of untruth. My fantasy was fulfilled, but a new one had taken its place— one that involved exploring the wildcat in her. Only now, I was a smarter Ian. I knew that some fantasies were left unspoken, and obsession could easily lead to ruin.

Sensing my lie, Emily frowned. "You think so? I hope so. Because like I said Friday, that's it for me. It was an amazing night, but my fantasies have been fulfilled. I don't need to go back there again."

"Neither do I." Part of me wondered if she really believed that, or like me she knew to play it safe. Either way, it didn't matter. I had her again, and I wasn't going risk losing her.

I reached for her hands, emotion clogging my throat when I tried to speak. I saw that emotion reflected in the shimmer of Emily's eyes. "I love you, Em. I was...I was so afraid I'd lost you."

"That could never happen."

I couldn't shake the smile from my face. She was right, and I'd been so focused on myself to realize it. No matter what, Emily would always be with me. Even if she got swept away by Ray, she'd come back to me in the end. I finally realized what she'd been saying this whole damn time: this was an awakening shared by both of us.

"What are you going to say to Ray tomorrow at work?"

"I've been thinking about that. I have the time, so I'm taking the week off. I'm going to tell my boss I hurt myself over the weekend and I can't come in."

She really had been thinking about this. A sick part of me wanted to throw Ray in front of her just to see if she really could resist temptation. I spoke before I could stop myself.

"Do you really want to do that? Shouldn't you have some closure?"

Emily rolled her eyes, but I hope she knew I was mostly kidding. "I've had all the closure I need with Ray." She winked and squeezed my hand. "It's best this way."

"Good." I restrained that obsessive desire to push her. It was going to be hard to bury that fantasy.

Emily shook her head, seemingly baffled by me. "I'm surprised you can just walk away now. Just days ago all you could think about was me fucking another man, and now you're totally done with that?" She used that word naturally now, it just rolled off her tongue. "What happened?"

She knew me well. I redirected.

"Just started to feel like this was becoming less about us and more about you and Ray—"

"But it's always been about us."

"And I realized that—"

"That we might be turning into one of *those* couples?" Emily finished.

"*Those* couples?"

"You know, bringing other men into the bedroom. Or, I don't know, swinging or whatever." Despite her crazy threesome, I loved that Emily still blushed at this stuff.

I pushed on. "My point is that I was afraid that things went too far to fix. Like, I'd taken apart the TV to see if I could get a sharper image and now I couldn't put it back together."

That was mostly true. I'd come so close to destroying everything, and I hadn't. Time to cool things down.

"Am I a TV now?" Emily laughed. "Yeah, I understand. I don't want this to become our lives, either. It scared me. I lost control last night. I could see us slipping, you know? Into what our marriage could turn into if we unleashed that again. I married you because I love you. Last night was fun, but you're all I need."

What our marriage could turn into if we unleashed that again. I was instantly hard at the thought of it, and was happy to be sitting down.

I leaned across the table and kissed her. "I love you, Emily, and I would never want to do anything that would risk our family. If I lost you, I would lose my mind."

But we could do everything up to that line...

Stop it.

Focus.

"You're everything to me," I finished.

"And you are to me. I love you and our family with all my heart. Now let's go get the kids and be together as a family."

After those crazy weeks, Emily and I were closer than ever. I started to realize that had less to do with the illicit sex and a lot more to do with our openness. We were in a better place now. We talked more. We were more in love than ever before.

As for that night, we relived it many times, although we talked about it less and less. Emily took the week off, true to her word, and hadn't seen Ray since. Their chapter was over.

It became easier to dampen down my obsession with the naughty Emily—Emily the hotwife. As events with Ray receded into memory, it was easy to pretend it was just a blip in Emily's otherwise proper sexuality, rather than a glimpse at something buried.

I almost was able to believe it. I came so close.

end

AN EXCERPT FROM
BECAUSE HE'S WATCHING
by Kirsten McCurran

Chapter One

Looking back now, I think I can pinpoint the moment when my marriage really changed. At the time, I didn't think anything of it. Ian, my husband, came home late one evening after a particularly tough day at work. His team had blown a meeting and—feeling sorry for himself—he'd gone out drinking afterward. I love my husband dearly, but sometimes I wish he had more confidence. He's a good man, a good father to our two kids, but sometimes I feel like he doesn't know how much I appreciate him, although I try to tell him every day.

At first, I was just angry that he'd driven drunk, but he started coming on to me—not unusual when he drinks, and he melted my defenses. Like I said, I still love Ian as much as I ever have and I still find him sexy after twelve years of marriage. He was the first man I really felt I could be myself with and let all my barriers down. I don't think enough women take that into account when picking a guy. Ian's handsome, tall and slender with dark hair, but maybe not as much of it now that he's in his early forties, but do any of us look like we did when we were twenty-five? I go to the gym almost every day, but when I look in the mirror I still only see what I'd like to fix, not what I've achieved. So Ian may not be the hottest guy on the planet, but he'll always be the sexiest guy to me.

Ian kissed me with a passion I had not felt in a long, long time and it took my breath away. I ignored the beer on his breath and pressed my body to his and felt he was already getting hard. His unusual spontaneity was hot and, before I knew it, I was leading him to the bedroom. Luckily, I'd just put the kids down. We were barely in the bedroom when he slipped his hand into the back of my boy shorts and groped my ass. I giggled and let him enjoy himself. I'd put a lot of work into that butt and I was glad he appreciated it. I said his name as I turned around and melted into his arms for another hot kiss, my tongue slipping into his mouth. Ian's desire was heating me up very quickly.

I was already dressed for bed, so I didn't have much to strip off. I peeled my snug cami away and I'd barely thrown it onto the bed before Ian was grabbing me. He massaged my breasts, easily bringing my long nipples to taut stiffness. It was weird, but it felt like he was touching me for the first time, like he couldn't get enough of me. I didn't know where this new eagerness came from, but I liked it.

After I shimmied out of my boy shorts, Ian eased me backward and I sat on the edge of the bed while he went to his knees. He kissed my breasts all over, like he was trying to kiss each of the tiny freckles that dotted my chest. My breasts are not huge, they're full B's, but I'm proud that they are still perky and draw attention, even at my age. I've caught the guys at the office checking them out when they think I'm not looking. As long as they behave, I don't mind the attention. I can admit it, part of me even likes it. Those guys would love to see me the way Ian was at that moment. I'm not the kind of woman who likes to show off, but the thought gave me the shivers, especially when combined with the way Ian was kissing and sucking my breasts. My nipples are so sensitive, and he knows just how to touch me to get me warm and moaning. But he was only teasing. Once I whimpered his name, he started kissing down my belly and pushed me onto my back.

"Oooo…yesss…" I moaned when he kissed my pussy. I propped up on my elbows so I could watch him and there was this incredible fire in his eyes. That was the first time I noticed something really different about my husband. Ian had me so wet, and when he pushed two fingers into me I cried out. His tongue moved rapidly and as he curved those fingers to hit my g-spot, he had me cumming easily. AH! AH!" I cried out before remembering the kids and biting my lip to quiet down.

I was panting as Ian kissed his way up my body and I spread my legs for him. I don't know when he lost his pants, but he pushed inside me and I cried out as he filled me. He took me quickly, with strong thrusts, filling me completely and I closed my eyes, sinking into the wonderful sensations of our love making.

"Let's turn," Ian whispered to me.

It felt good and I didn't want him to stop. I groaned when he pulled out of me and we both moved up on the bed. This was new. We did not usually switch positions in the middle. But as I took him back inside me I didn't mind the interruption anymore. I love to be on top, because I can control everything and make sure I get my climax, even draw it out if I want to. And besides, I get the added benefit of Ian playing with me while I ride him. He kneaded my breasts as I rode him and he looked up at me lustily and I would have loved to have known what was going through his head.

"Oh, Ian…" I sighed when he leaned forward and kissed my breast. He hungrily sucked my nipple between his lips then chased it with his tongue, sending a charge through me, right down to my pussy. I fell forward, holding his head to my chest as my pussy clenched around him and my grip tightened and I rode him harder.

He sucked on my other nipple and my breathing grew heavier as I gasped with pleasure and whimpered his name.

I pulled Ian into a hard kiss to muffle my growing moans. He grabbed my butt and pulled me into him and the bed creaked beneath us as we slammed together. We worked up a sweat and my nipples slid along his slick chest, the simple touch making me crazy. I was getting close, so close. Ian found the sweet spot on my neck and nibbled. It was like he was devouring me and I cried out, my entire body tightening as my orgasm was just on the horizon now. I pushed him away and arched my back, slamming my pussy onto him and ran my fingers through my long, dark, sweat-slick hair.

"Uhhh…Ian…Ian…" I cried as my world tilted like a ship on rough seas. I came so hard and I wanted Ian to cum with me. "Cum, Ian! Cum now, please!" I demanded. He exploded inside me and my muscles drained every last drop from him.

I rolled off of Ian and lay on my back, staring at the ceiling. Wow! That had been amazing! I turned to tell him so, but my husband—exhausted from our lovemaking, and all the beer he'd had—was already falling asleep. I just smiled and shook my head and then padded into the bathroom to clean up. Something had gotten into Ian that night, but I had no idea what. I would have thought he'd visited a strip club, if he was that kind of guy. Whatever it was, I couldn't complain. But little did I know that it was the beginning of a huge change in our marriage.

***

After that intense night of sex, things returned to normal for a few days. I could tell Ian was looking at me differently, but he didn't say anything about it. I figured it was just a phase and tried to ignore it. With two kids to take care of and a full plate at work, I just didn't have time to worry about what was going on in my husband's head.

Ian wasn't the only one acting differently. Ray, one of my co-workers, was suddenly paying me more attention as well. It was the oddest thing. I felt like my breasts had grown two sizes. I know I had an extra bounce in my step the morning after that hot night with Ian. Ray seemed to notice something different about me right away.

"Looks like someone got lucky last night," he joked when we met by the coffee machine.

"Maybe," I smiled knowingly.

I wasn't offended by his comment. We'd had a pretty flirty relationship from the time he started at the company, about a year ago. It was nice, to have a handsome younger man show an interest, even if it just was harmless fun. I've never been the woman that guys like Ray take an interest in. Those guys always go for the flashy blonde, with the big chest. That is certainly not me. I've always been the "cute" one, the girl guys want to take home to their mother, not the one they want to get down and dirty with. My thick, dark hair falls past my shoulders and a light dusting of freckles dapples my cheeks. People look at me and just think I'm the innocent, good girl. I'm petite, and going to the gym keeps my figure tight. I've been told more than once that I look younger than the thirty-six I am. But it's not in me to flaunt what I've got, not too much anyway. The sexy little things I do, I do for myself and sometimes I fantasize about being that bad girl no one expects. Only Ian knows that side of me.

Ray was about ten years or so younger than me, and built in a way that gets women mentally undressing a man. I could tell right away by how his shirts stretched over his broad chest and how his slacks hugged his butt that this man took care of himself. That was confirmed when I started seeing him at the same gym I attended during my lunch hour. So if this handsome, young hunk wanted to flirt with me, who was I to stop him?

"Really? There's still some fire left in the old furnace?" He sounded surprised.

"What do you mean?"

"Just you don't see women who've been married as long as you come into work smiling like you are."

I laughed. "Not all marriages turn into monotony and boredom, Ray." Although I had to admit, before that night things had gotten somewhat routine. "And besides, there are plenty of things about me that would surprise you, dear."

"Oh, I'm sure," he replied and I'm sure he was checking out my butt as I left the break room.

It wasn't the first time I caught him sneaking a peek, but it was the first time he was so open about it. I flushed, but smiled and hoped he enjoyed the view. The gray slacks I wore really did show off my butt. The rest of that day Ray found more excuses than usual to come around my cubicle and talk and he made a few more comments about how I must be bored after being with the same man for so long. I assured him that I loved my husband, but that didn't mean I never had other thoughts.

"I mean, I'm not dead, right? Ian is a wonderful and loving husband, but girls like to look around just like guys do. Sometimes I'll see a hot young guy and have a thought or two." I couldn't believe I was telling him that, but he had worn me down throughout the day.

"You've got to tell me more, Emily."

"I don't have to do anything of the kind, Ray. And you'd better get back to work before someone notices you're not doing anything. Just use your imagination." God only knows what he was imagining, but a huge smile spread across his face. I knew that handsome, charming smile well and, I'll admit, it made my heart skip a beat knowing he might be thinking something dirty about me. Is it awful that I was teasing him like that? I don't think so.

***

A couple days later, everyone was headed out for Happy Hour after work and Ray insisted I join them. It was not a surprise. He'd kept up his extra attention for the past few days, coming on strong. I tried to explain I had to get home to take care of the kids, but he wouldn't take no for an answer. He was like the Pied Piper and I couldn't resist his tune. Deciding there was no harm in one drink, I left Ian a message and let him know I would be late and said not to hold dinner. Besides, I hadn't gone out with the guys from work in ages, I told myself. It had *nothing* to do with Ray's insistence.

It was nice to be out with everyone and have a couple glasses of wine. Sometimes, you just need to feel like an adult in your own right, not someone's wife, someone's mother. I hope that doesn't sound terrible, but sometimes you need some time for yourself. We hit one of the usual haunts, an Irish pub called McGinty's. It was large, but felt intimate because of all the dark wood and brass rails and red upholstery. The place was crowded with a lot of hedge fund and banking types when we arrived, but the six of us found a corner for ourselves at the end of the bar. I ordered a glass of merlot, which brought ribbing from the others, who were all guys. They treated me like an equal, which made me proud since the office was quite the boys' club. I'm the only woman in our department who's not an administrative assistant.

The crowd made it hot in the bar and I slipped off my jacket, putting it over the back of my stool, and opened an extra button on my blouse. I didn't realize how much that exposed me until I caught Ray looking down my blouse when I leaned forward to pick up my glass. With the way Ray had been behaving the last couple days I had to resist the urge to pull my blouse closed—I didn't want to give him any real encouragement. But then, it would be obvious I knew he was looking if I just buttoned it back up, I told myself. And if I'm honest, I liked the way he had been looking at me the past couple days. If a hot younger guy like Ray was showing so much interest then I must still have it.

I probably shouldn't have hit the wine like that after having such a light lunch, because naughty thoughts crept into my head. *Just how much could he see*, I wondered. Could he see the lacy edge of my black Victoria's Secret bra? Did he like the cleavage it created? And is it bad that I wanted him to? It was just harmless fun, right? That's what I told myself, anyway.

Sexy lingerie is something I'd started indulging in over the past few years. When I got back into shape after having our son Davy, I wanted to do something to show how good I felt about myself. It makes me feel sexy to wear something silky and frilly underneath the business clothes I have to wear for work every day. It's like a secret I have that all those guys around me have no idea about. The lightly-padded bras give me a little boost, and hide my sensitive nipples, and the thigh-highs I've taken to wearing just make me feel naughty. If only those guys knew! Sometimes, I wished Ian took more notice of it, especially the thigh-highs. He always used to try to talk me into wearing them, but I just felt silly. Now that I'm little older and more confident I like it and don't care if it's not practical. Unfortunately, my husband takes less notice of such things now that we've been married for so long. I don't think he ever notices what I wear to work, which is when I am the most dressed-up.

As we talked, I noticed a couple of the other guys were sneaking peeks too, and I've got to say, it had an effect on me. I might have even leaned forward more than I needed to. As long as I pretended not to notice, there was no awkwardness. I blamed my feelings on Ray's heightened attention. I sat on one of the high stools with my legs crossed and he stood behind me, over my right shoulder. He kept putting his hands on my arms and pressing against me when he leaned in to grab his beer from the bar and I started to get worried that the others might notice. The last thing I wanted was to put an idea into those guys' perverted heads, but I was trapped and didn't have much of a choice. At the end of my second glass of wine, I wasn't as worried about it and just enjoyed it.

The others filtered out until it was just me and Ray. He sat next to me with his hand on mine as it rested on the bar. As we talked, he kept glancing down and I blushed furiously when I realized he could see the lacy top of my stocking. I wore a snug pencil skirt that came to the knee, which was safe, but it had a small slit on the side. The way I sat with my legs crossed had pulled it open. I didn't even want to know what he was thinking now.

"It's good to have you out with us," Ray said. "We don't see much of you."

"It's tough to balance having two kids with having a real life. It's like my real work begins when I get home at night. Work is almost a break." I laughed.

"But you do need some time to enjoy yourself. Do you and uhh…"

"Ian." Did he intentionally forget my husband's name?

"Ian, right. Do you and Ian ever get out for date night?"

"Not often, but we have plenty of time for ourselves. Don't worry about us."

"On Demand movies on the couch. Exciting!" Ray teased.

"It gets more exciting than that. Don't you think married people have sex?"

"In the beginning, sure, but it falls off over time. I've got to be honest, I know that I'm not ready to swear that I'll only ever have sex with one person for the rest of my life."

"I'm not going to give you details, but Ian and I have a great sex life. And if you love someone then they are all you need," I answered. "I guess you haven't truly been in love yet."

Ray laughed. "Maybe, maybe not. All I am saying is that forever is a long time, and when someone is still young and hot like you, well, sometimes it's got to be hard for you to walk the straight-and-narrow."

"Ray! Stop it!" I chided. It was the first time he'd ever come right out and said he thinks I'm hot. I must have turned three shades of red.

"A beautiful woman like you should be used to taking compliments." He squeezed my hand, then nodded toward my empty glass. "Would you like another?"

The last glass of wine had been my third and I had a buzz on, so yet another one was not a good idea. I checked my watch and couldn't believe how late it was. Ian must have been ready to send out a search party.

"I really need to get going. The trains only run every hour this late, and I've got a walk to the station from here."

"Don't be silly. I'll drive you home."

"Ray, it's too far," I protested. "It's got to be a least a half hour drive each way. I can't ask you to do that." I knew he had a condo in the city.

"You're not asking. I want to, and I don't take no for an answer."

He paid the bill and pulled the stool away from the bar so I could hop down. I took my purse and jacket, but left the latter off because it was a warm evening. He took my arm in his during the walk back to the parking garage, a very gentlemanly, even romantic, gesture. Ray was so solid. It was the first time I'd ever actually touched him, except to shake hands, and his arm was like stone. It was like being walked down the street by some Greek sculpture. Except Ray was clothed, I thought naughtily. I leaned into him as we walked, enjoying his strength.

Ray held the door of his expensive, black Mercedes coupe and I felt quite elegant as I slid into the buttery-soft leather seat. I know he got both a glimpse down my blouse and at my stocking top, but by that point, I didn't mind. All that wine, combined with being out with a handsome young man, had taken a toll. I was very horny and couldn't wait to get home to Ian. He was in for quite a treat. It would be my way of paying him back for when he came home all sexed up the other night.

The expensive black sports car made easy work of the roads, gliding in an out of traffic. Ray worked the six-speed transmission like a master and squeezed every ounce of power out of the softly purring engine. He controlled the sleek vehicle so easily that I couldn't help but think of how easily he could take control in other areas.

I told Ray he only had to run me to the train station because I'd left the car there, but he wanted to take me home. He said he wasn't sure I should be driving, but I felt fine by the time we were back out in the suburbs. He kept checking me out in the darkened car, and I think he just wanted to keep me with him a little longer. He wasn't the only one. I kept looking over through the shifting shadows and watched his strong jaw and those stormy eyes. It was like I was in the car with my very own action hero.

It might have been a sudden attack of conscious for the heavy flirting I'd been doing all night. That, and I didn't know how my husband would feel if he saw I was being dropped off at home by another man, so when we turned onto my street, I asked Ray to stop a few houses down from ours.

"Tonight was great. You really need to come out more," Ray said, setting the parking brake.

"It was fun. I'll definitely come out whenever I can get away." Just thinking about going home to all that chaos my kids create put a damper on me. Sitting in that car with Ray, I was an exotic, dangerous woman. Back in the house, I was mom.

"Don't wait too long. You know I won't be around much longer and you'll miss me when I'm gone." There was that smile again.

"Maybe," I replied coyly and unlocked the seatbelt.

I leaned over to kiss Ray on the cheek, but he caught me and guided my lips to his. I was so stunned that I did nothing at first. But he held me there, fingers tousling my hair, and his lips were so insistent that I weakened and kissed him back. We probably only kissed for a handful of seconds, but it felt like forever. Suddenly the car was so hot I could hardly stand it. Ray's lips were soft, but there was a power there and I would have gone weak in the knees if I hadn't been sitting. Only when I felt his tongue slipping between my lips did I come to my senses. He let me pull away and I fell back into my seat, breathless.

"Ray! I'm married! Why did you…" I stammered, gathering my things and reaching for the door latch.

"I'm sorry, Emily. I couldn't help myself, and I thought I was picking up signals."

"I was not sending you any signals!"

"Emily…"

"Listen, I've got to go. My husband and kids are waiting for me."

I swung out of the car, slammed the door, and immediately saw Ian and the kids in front of the house. It looked like they were just coming home. I plastered a smile on my face and waved to Ray as he drove away. I didn't want Ian thinking anything was amiss. But beneath that smile, I was a mess. God, how was I going to face Ray in the office? How the hell had that happened?

It only took the short walk to the front door for my outrage to wear off and my smile to become genuine. Maybe I had sent out some mixed signals, but I blamed it on the wine. And what a kiss! It was so hot! Ray said, *he couldn't help himself!* A guy like him wanted to kiss me, and couldn't help himself! By the time I reached my family I was glowing and thinking I couldn't get Ian alone fast enough.

"Mommy," Jenny shouted, as she charged into my arms. I scooped her up and walked over to Ian, who had the oddest look on his face. It was like he'd just eaten something bad. I kissed him longer and with more passion than I usually would in front of the kids.

"How's my favorite family?" I asked.

Ian didn't answer and storm clouds crossed his face when I bent down to put Jenny on the ground. I was sure he looked down my blouse and I thought I must be sexy if even my husband is checking me out like that. Still, he had that strange look, and for the first time in our marriage I couldn't tell what he was thinking. Did he see Ray as he drove away and was angry? Why would he be? Ian couldn't have seen Ray make the pass at me, and even if he had, he's not usually the jealous type. Actually, he's proven to be the opposite over the years. I was just projecting my own guilt onto him, I decided. Or maybe not.

"Who dropped you off, hon?" Ian asked, pointedly nonchalant.

"Just a co-worker," I said, and felt my pale cheeks flushing. "I had one glass of wine too many, so he did me a favor."

"Anyone I know?" he asked, smiling.

"I'm not sure. I don't think you and Ray have met." I felt guilty just saying the name, and I realized that his mouth may have been smiling, but his eyes were blank.

"He's quite a gentleman, offering to drop you off," Ian replied, putting his arm around me while we walked. His smile did not reach his eyes.

"You're not jealous, are you?" I met his eyes for the first time and felt like he could see right through me.

I didn't know what to say, so I replied, "To be continued," and busied myself with the children.

Ian watched me closely as I went about putting the kids to bed. Was he looking for something specific? Did he see Ray kiss me and think I did something to encourage it? I might have, but at that moment, I wasn't ready to be that honest with myself. Ray and I had always flirted, and I don't know that I did anything tonight to make him think it was okay to kiss me.

"What?" I finally asked, bent over to put the diaper bag away.

"Watching you in that outfit, I'm beginning to wish I worked with you."

"Really?" I replied, relieved that he wasn't jealous. He was horny. Whatever had a hold of him the other night must have come back. I laughed. "You letch. Do I need to file a sexual harassment complaint?"

Ian pulled me to my feet and into his arms. "You'd be complaining, would you?"

"You're pretty sure of yourself," I smiled.

He responded by pulling me tighter, so I could feel his hard-on through his pants.

"Yeah, this is definitely sexual harassment," I giggled.

"Oh, come on. Don't tell me guys haven't ever come onto you. I'm sure that guy Ray and you have flirted a little."

Was Ian psychic? I was worried for a second, but from his smile and his erection, I knew that he wasn't angry and jealous. It slowly dawned on me. Ian was turned on by seeing another man drop me off at home. He thought I looked sexy, and he liked that maybe the guys around my office thought so too. I was shocked, but I shouldn't have been. After what happened last year, it's not like it was without precedent.

"Maybe… I think we should discuss this in my office," I replied and smiled slyly.

The bedroom door was barely closed before Ian was on top of me. I attacked him just as ferociously, pulling at his shirt while he fumbled with the buttons on my blouse.

"Uhhh…honey…it feels so good…" I whimpered as I pulled his cock out of his jeans.

Our legs tangled and we tumbled onto the bed together, groping and furiously kissing each other. All of that sexual tension with Ray came bubbling to the surface. I couldn't remember the last time I wanted Ian so badly. I was already soaked down below and couldn't wait to get him inside me. Was it terrible that another man's attention had me dying to make love to my husband?

He hiked up my skirt, almost tearing it at the slit, and wrenched my thong to the side. He rammed his cock in me and I gasped at the feeling of being instantly filled. He gripped my thigh, right over my stocking top, and took me forcefully. It was even more intense than the other night and I couldn't help but think of Ray. I know he's the type of man who takes his women. I could just imagine him hiking up my skirt and taking me the way that Ian was. I knotted my fingers in his hair, pulling, like I was pulling him into me. His weight pressed onto me, pinning me to the bed, and all of the sudden, I climaxed. I threw my body back at Ian's as the orgasm ripped through me.

"Do it, lover…do it…Ian…ahhh…"

I felt him cum inside me then fully collapse onto my body, burying his face in the spill of my dark hair. I loved this fiery, passionate version of my husband, but I was dying to know where it was coming from.

"What got into you?" I asked.

"Mm, maybe I should ask, what got into *you?*" He kept me pinned to the bed, our faces inches apart. "Your gentleman suitor maybe?"

"Ray? Ian, don't be silly…" I turned my face away from his, not wanting my hazel eyes to betray anything.

"It is!" Ian said, almost triumphantly.

Then I felt Ian stiffen inside me, and it cemented my thought before. The idea of me being attracted to another man excited my husband. I didn't know how to feel about that. Should I be angry? "Thinking about me and Ray turns you on, doesn't it?" I asked.

"Maybe a little. That's weird, isn't it?"

Instead of answering him, I followed my impulses and kissed Ian. It was a slow, sensual kiss that turned increasingly passionate and I felt him twitch inside me. Our tongues fought and he was fully hard again. That was impressive recovery time. He rolled off of me and his hard cock slipped out with a slurp. I missed him inside of me. I was as ready for round two as he was.

"Do you always dress like that for work?" Ian asked.

I looked back over my shoulder, thick, chestnut hair veiling my face as I stood. "Do you mean like this?" I asked. I pulled my skirt down and it smoothed across my butt as I bent forward to give him the best view. His eyes widened when I turned, giving him the same peek at my thigh-high that Ray got back in the bar. Did Ray like it as much as my husband did? The thought made me tingle all over.

"I think it would look even better like this," Ian said, and reached over to draw down the zipper over my butt. He winked and I wiggled, letting the skirt drop to the floor. I felt so sexy standing there in just my shirt and high heels, with my thigh-highs exposed. He ran his fingers over the exposed flesh above my stocking, making me quiver.

"This is just like Bobby's wedding, isn't it?" I asked in a breathy whisper. We'd never talked about that night, but that was why it wasn't such a shock that Ian was turned on by seeing Ray drop me off.

A year ago, we had attended the wedding of Ian's nephew. Ian had just injured his knee and was stuck at our table all night, sipping beers. Being the loving husband he is, he encouraged me to dance with others because I love to dance. At first I said no, I would stick to his side, but he insisted, so when one of the groomsmen asked me, I joined him on the dance floor. He was a handsome younger man in his mid-twenties and a great dancer, but I felt guilty about dancing with him, so as soon as the song ended I returned to Ian to make sure he wasn't jealous. He insisted he wasn't and told me to go back out there and have fun. I ended up staying out there for much of the night, fueled by seemingly endless glasses of wine and the enthusiasm of all the younger men there. It was like I was passed from one handsome, younger man to another, to another, and to another. Soon, my head was spinning with mixed emotions. I enjoyed being in the arms of these fun guys. It took me back to a time when I was younger and single and carefree.

But as the night wore on, I danced with one of the guys more than the others. His name was Kyle, and he was tall and buff, very much like Ray, actually. He looked achingly handsome in his tuxedo, and it was exciting that he wanted to dance with me. I felt so sexy in his arms and, after stopping him the first few times, I eventually let his hands stray to my butt. I wasn't thinking about my husband as I laid my head on his broad chest and closed my eyes. I was thinking about how he would look out of that tux.

I only returned to Ian when the music ended, and I was sure he would be angry. But no. There was a fire in his eyes like I'd never seen before. We went back to our room and had the hottest sex since our honeymoon, and Ian watched me like I was a sex goddess as I rode him. I couldn't help but think that I wanted Kyle to look at me that way. It was the first time I wanted someone other than Ian to see my inner sex kitten. It was an incredible night, but we never did discuss why we were both so horny. I think we were both too embarrassed.

"Yeah. It turned you on too, didn't it?" Ian said.

"You know it did, but I was worried of what you thought of me." I was so aroused that night. I went on pure instinct, never pausing to think about what could happen.

"You didn't know? Can you read my mind now?"

I looked down at his raging hard-on as I peeled off my blouse. "I don't think I need to. But do I really want to know what you were thinking that night?"

Ian looked chagrined. "Probably not."

Half-turning, I unclasped my bra and tossed it on the bed and saw Ian was focused on my breasts. Sometimes I think he loves my chest the best. The erotic tension in the bedroom was electric.

"Does that guy who dropped you off ever flirt with you? I mean, you are a beautiful woman."

"A beautiful, *married* woman. But yes, sometimes we flirt. He's just one of those guys. Does it turn you on?" I cupped my breasts and shivered as I touched my nipples.

Ian pulled off his remaining clothes and watched me from the edge of the bed. "Maybe. Is it just flirting?"

"Do you want to know how serious it is?" I played with my thong as I spoke, watching him carefully. It was the first time we'd ever explored this, and I thought my heart was going to beat out of my chest. "Are you asking if it's more than just *harmless* flirting? Does Ray ever push it?"

"Emily…" He looked anguished, but he was harder than ever.

"What do you want to know? Do you want to know if he makes passes at me?" I rolled down my thong and straddled him. I was so slick from our first quickie that he slid right into me. It felt so good.

"Does he?"

"Yes. He tried to kiss me tonight," I whispered. I could feel Ray's lips on mine again and I tightened around my husband.

"You knew he wanted you, and you let him drive you home." Ian gripped my hips and surged inside me.

"Yes. I'm a big girl, I can handle myself. Ohhh, Ian…" I started rocking back and forth on him.

"And he kissed you…"

"He tried, but I stopped him," I moaned. *After a moment*, I thought. We started moving faster and I thought about the hunger in Ray's kiss. I could feel how much he wanted me, the way Ian wanted me now. Somehow, Ray saw that side of me I reserve only for my husband. It excited *and* scared me.

I couldn't be sure, but it was almost like Ian breathed the word, *why*. He said, "I love you, Emily."

"I love you too, honey." A wave of guilt swamped me. How could I feel those things about Ray. It was so wrong! "I love you so much," I stressed.

"Show me," Ian moaned.

We consumed each other with a passion we rarely reached anymore. It was something we shared only when we'd been parted, or when we connected on a deep, deep level, which was so rare with the kids and our obligations. We made love with the intensity we did that night after Bobby's wedding, when I thought of Kyle and I know Ian was thinking of me *with* Kyle. We clawed at each other, lips smearing across each other as we each fought to control the kiss and our coupling. As I came into the home stretch, I pushed him onto his back and rode hard as he dug his fingers into my plush ass, pulling me into him. I slammed up and down on him and quickly reached a rare peak.

"Oh God! Oh God!" Ian cried underneath me as he came.

"Yes! Yes! Yes!" I breathed, oddly quiet as I came. I ran my fingers through his chest hair and then slumped forward. He buried his face in my breasts and we slowly came down from our high.

Later, when we lay in bed together, naked, Ian finally spoke.

"You know, I was thinking…"

"Don't hurt yourself," I laughed. It felt good to laugh. The tension was gone.

"I think we should meet up for Happy Hour sometime."

"Sure, it would be fun," I said.

"*And* maybe we could pretend to be strangers?" It was more question than statement. I know he was feeling me out.

"Pretend to be strangers? So you can come in and hit on me?" I couldn't suppress my giggles. My first thought was that he was being silly, but then I warmed to the idea. It could be fun. And maybe it was a way to explore this vague fantasy we both seemed to have.

"You think I'm crazy," he said, looking away.

I kissed him. "I'm game. When?"

Ian beamed. "How about Friday after work? I've heard good things about this place called Bar 88."

This excerpt comes courtesy of Kirsten McCurran. If you'd like to read more about Emily's side of the story, you can find Because He's Watching *at all major online book retailers, including Amazon, Barnes & Noble, and Apple's iBookstore.*

ACKNOWLEDGEMENTS

This book wouldn't have happened without the encouragement and collaboration of Kirsten McCurran. Way back in 2011, when I began what would become this book, Kirsten was so intrigued by it that she starting exploring Emily's side of their adventure. She went on to publish Emily's story in *Because He's Watching*. Ian's story did not. At the time, I wasn't comfortable with the character I'd created—a man so obsessed with his wife-watching fantasy that it drove him to do some questionable things. Two years later, I still don't think I'd be the guy's friend, but I'm at peace with who he is as a character—and a compelling one at that.

If you're looking for more of the story in a Tarantino sort of way, check out *Because He's Watching*. You'll read everything you just read from Emily's perspective. And if you're *really* patient, maybe you'll get to read the next chapter in Emily and Ian's adventure.

Okay, acknowledgements now:

Lucy V. Morgan, of course, editor extraordinaire; she's doesn't just keep my plots, characters, grammar, and spelling in check, but she's a great friend;

Kirsten McCurran, of course, for obvious enough reasons that I'm not going to bother repeating here;

My beta readers, Max, Jake, and Stephen, who've made sure that I'm not completely off the rails;

My wife for supporting me—not just by giving me time to write, but for being such a kick-ass woman in my life.

And thanks to all of you for buying the book (and taking time to read this far). If you liked it, leave a review, tell a friend, or tell me if you want, you can reach me at kennywright.writer@gmail.com. Cheers!

ABOUT THE AUTHOR

I'm just a guy who writes what I like to read: steamy, explicit erotica that's just crazy enough to be true. I write romantic erotica. I write about characters that I like, and endings that feel natural. I write stories where husbands watch their wives get naughty. I write about MILFs and erotic games and loss of innocence. I believe in a world where men read and appreciate erotica, and hope to contribute to it word by word.

Find me online at www.kennywriter.com, or follow me on Twitter at @kennywriter.

BOOKS BY KENNY WRIGHT

Unconventional: Business Meets Pleasure

Does what happens in Vegas, stay in Vegas, when it involves Adam's sexy older boss? Blonde, European, and three pay-grades above his own, Linnea Sorenson was untouchable. Until she wasn't.

Traveling to Las Vegas for the Health & Fitness Convention, Linnea and Adam are from different castes. He's a worker bee who works the convention floor, she shmoozes with her executive colleagues. In ordinary circumstances, any overlap would be all business, and any pleasure would be kept in check. But Vegas is no ordinary place. What started as a game of control leads to a loss of it for one, and agonizing pleasure for them both.

Find out what happens when events at this convention take a turn for the unconventional.

Something Forbidden

Wife-watching. Swinging. Consensual infidelity. These are not concepts that Maxwell Callahan understands, let alone fantasizes about. Max has a great life: husband, father, successful bar owner. He has no plans to shake it up.

And then he witnesses a couple play a dangerous game of pick-up in his bar: the wife gets picked up, the husband watches. A seed takes root and starts to grow. What would it be like to watch his beautiful wife, Katie, in the same situation?

Smart, successful, yet a little conservative, he never thought Katie would ever entertain such an idea…until she does. This suburban couple is about to take a wild ride as they turn fantasy into reality. Don't miss this marital adventure as Katie and Max try something forbidden.

Just Watch Me

Dean and Danielle have been playing their game for the past year now: they'd enter a bar as strangers and see what happens. Sometimes, Dean "picked" her up. Other times, he sat back and watched her flirt with other men. And every time, they ended the night together, their passion rekindled.

Jealousy and excitement warred within Dean, but the thrill was becoming too great to ignore. For Danielle, the game had awoken feelings within her she thought long buried–feelings that scared as much as they excited.

Then came the Hawaii trip. Hundreds of miles from home, was this the opportunity to take things further than they'd ever dared? When a stranger approaches Danielle at the swanky bar, full of surfer-swagger and sun-kissed good looks, the answer was clear.

All In: Strip Poker Done Right

Play strip poker? Ben never thought he would. Not with his wife, Amy, and especially not with their asshole friend, Scott. Lawyers all three, they were more likely to strip their opponents of pride, not clothing.

Not that Ben wasn't intrigued—especially in the company of two attractive couples with a history of flirtation. He'd love to see either woman naked; he just wasn't sure how he felt about the guys ogling his wife. But when the wine begins to flow, inhibitions loosen, and clothes start coming off, he discovers a part of himself that's turned on by the attention Amy commands.

Soon, the three couples are caught in the throes of high-stakes poker. Secrets come out, things get wild, and Ben discovers a side of his wife he never knew existed.

Leap

On February 29, a day that comes just once every four years, Jack Carter announces that, "What happens on Leap Day stays on Leap Day." His wife Sarah knows he's up to something, and when he explains that today is a day to take risks and get a little crazy, she grasps what it is: he wants to watch her with another man.

Jack had the fantasy first; and at first, Sarah didn't understand it. Hell, neither did Jack. All he knew was that the thought of his wife in the arms of another man was exciting; the build-up, the flirtation, the act, even his nauseous jealousy always got him hard. Sarah didn't deny her own arousal, especially when her coworker, David, began taking the role of imagined lover. He was fit, hot, and most importantly, he was attracted to her.

Neither Jack nor Sarah ever thought they'd take the plunge from reality to fantasy. It was too risky. Too crazy. With February 29 just beginning, will it be the day they finally make the leap?

Also by Kenny Wright

After School Special (A Short)
Eight Hundred Dollar Heels (A Short)
Moving Mrs. Mitchell (A Short)
Naughty But Nice (A Short)
Rediscovering Danielle (A Short)
While She Watches

For a full list of titles, along with their covers, synopses, and where to purchase, go to www.kennywriter.com/books.